FINESSING CLARISSA

Amy and Effy Tribble place this advertisement in the *Morning Post* and hire themselves out as chaperones to prepare difficult young misses for marriage, educating them in their School of Manners. Lovely, wealthy and well bred, Clarissa Vevian has been unable to find a suitable husband because of her terrible clumsiness. Her petite and fastidious mother has tried to mould Clarissa into a dainty miss to fit the fashion – but all her efforts are doomed to failure. And when Clarissa enters the Tribble sisters' home, they fear their reputation for matchmaking success may be destroyed – along with their carpets and furniture!

FINESSING CLARISSA

FINESSING CLARISSA

by

M. C. Beaton

Magna Large Print Books
Long Preston, North Yorkshire,
BD23 4ND, England.

British Library Cataloguing in Publication Data.

Beaton, M. C.
 Finessing Clarissa.

 A catalogue record of this book is
 available from the British Library

 ISBN 978-0-7505-3762-9

This edition is published by Canvas,
an imprint of Constable & Robinson Ltd., 2012

Published in Large Print 2013 by arrangement with
Constable & Robinson Ltd.

Magna Large Print is an imprint of Library Magna Books Ltd.

Printed and bound in Great Britain by
T.J. (International) Ltd., Cornwall, PL28 8RW

1

Disasters come not singly,
But as if they watched and waited,
Scanning one another's motions,
When the first descends, the others
Follow, follow, gathering flock-wise
Round their victim sick and wounded—
First a shadow, then a sorrow,
Till the air is dark with anguish.

Longfellow

The tall house in Holles Street was filled with the sounds of bustle and activity as the Tribble sisters prepared for the arrival of the Honourable Clarissa Vevian, daughter of Viscount and Viscountess Clarendon.

Clarissa was the Tribbles' latest client, for the sisters were in business, and that business was to school seemingly impossible young ladies and make them fit to take their place at the London Season and find a husband.

Amy and Effy Tribble, spinster twins in

straitened circumstances, had hit upon the idea of advertising for 'difficult' girls. They had been very successful with their three latest charges but had feared they would never get another. No parent wanted to let the polite world know that their daughter was so impossibly unmarriageable that they had to hire outside help.

Effy, silver-haired and dainty, was still in a state of happy euphoria at the prospect of having a new charge to bring out. Amy Tribble, horsey and mannish, was beginning to be plagued with worries. It was now well known that the girls they chaperoned were difficult. So what was up with this Clarissa that had made her parents send her all the way from Bath to be schooled?

But she kept her doubts to herself. If she voiced them to Effy, then Effy would at first protest, then weep, and then take to her bed, leaving Amy with all the work of preparation.

Amy's gaunt and stern exterior belied a soft and feminine interior. She felt she would like a strong man to lean on. There was, of course, Mr Haddon, their old friend who had returned from India a rich nabob, but of late, Effy had more and more appropriated Mr Haddon as *her* property. Mr Haddon seemed quite charmed by Effy's flutterings and flirtatious ways and Amy felt rejected and unwanted.

'You will probably find there is nothing up with this Clarissa at all,' said Effy, arranging a bowl of spring flowers in a vase. 'I have not seen dear Georgina, her mother, you know, in this age, but she was a delicate, fairy-like creature. We have had our difficulties with the others, but it all turned out well, did it not?'

'After a great many hair-raising adventures and upsets,' pointed out Amy sourly. 'Our last charge was nearly raped but was saved by Yvette, who stabbed that rogue to death.' Yvette was the Tribbles' resident French dressmaker who had added to their worries by becoming pregnant by a Frenchman who had subsequently run off to France and left her.

'Oh, it will all be splendidly easy,' trilled Effy. 'Do you not remember Georgina?'

'Vaguely,' said Amy, stretching her legs and looking gloomily at her large feet. 'We've done so many Seasons ourselves, years and years of 'em.'

Effy frowned. She did not like to be reminded of all their failures. She maintained the fiction that their spinster state was by choice. She had been a plain girl and was

11

now a very pretty middle-aged woman, her sandy hair being now silvery-white and her figure trim.

'Mr Haddon,' announced the butler.

Effy snatched a flower out of the vase and held it to her cheek and assumed a dreamy pose.

'Won't do,' said Amy waspishly. 'You look silly.'

Mr Haddon was ushered in. He was a thin, spare man dressed in neat but plain clothes.

'All ready for your next client, ladies?' he asked.

'As ready as we'll ever be,' said Amy sourly, for Effy had put the flower back in the vase and was fluttering up to Mr Haddon.

Mr Haddon sat down and surveyed Amy's face with shrewd eyes. 'I shall just go and see if they know to serve those caraway cakes you like so much, Mr Haddon,' cooed Effy. Her dress had a short silk train at the back and Effy hoped Mr Haddon noticed the exquisite line of it as she left the room.

'Something is troubling you,' said Mr Haddon to Amy. 'What is it?'

'It's this girl, Clarissa,' said Amy, shifting restlessly. 'I haven't said anything to Effy because she would fuss so and then take to her bed. But I cannot help feeling there must be something really awful wrong with her. I mean, what kind of parents would send their daughter here, after there has been murder done in this house, if they were not absolutely desperate?'

'Now, Miss Amy, do not vex yourself. You know what the aristocracy is like. They turn their children over to the care of nurses and governesses from the day they are born and have little to do with them after that. You will probably find she is plain and did not take at the Bath assemblies and so has been sent to you.'

'The Viscount Clarendon is very rich,' said Amy. 'That means the girl's got a large dowry. When in this day and age did a girl with a large dowry have to have anything in the way of looks?'

'Well, perhaps she is a romantic and reads too many novels and falls in love with quite unsuitable beaux. That is easily corrected. You will find it is something manageable.'

'Trouble's coming to this house,' said Amy. 'I can feel it. When that Berkeley creature was murdered...'

'He was not murdered,' said Mr Haddon gently. 'He was killed by your brave dress-maker in order to save Delilah. Quite another thing.'

'Well, death. Anyway, I feel disaster is upon us.'

'The east wind is all that is upon us,' said Mr Haddon, 'and that always causes disorders of the spleen. Rally, Miss Amy. Rally!'

Amy grinned. 'You may have the right of it. I've been blue-devilled lately.'

'When does the Honourable Clarissa arrive?'

'This evening sometime, or so her parents said when they last wrote. They are not coming with her. She's been sent off with only her maid for company. Seems odd.'

'It is of no use worrying,' said Mr Haddon comfortably. 'We shall know what she is like soon enough.'

'Perhaps you might like to stay until she arrives?' asked Amy.

Mr Haddon had arranged to meet an old friend from India that evening at his club. But he took a look at Amy's anxious face, and said, 'Yes, of course I shall stay. I have a letter to send to a friend cancelling an engagement and then I shall be free.'

'If you would really rather go...'

'No, no, Miss Amy. I, too, am anxious to find out what Clarissa is like.'

Effy on her return was delighted to hear Mr Haddon had elected to stay. She rushed off again to order a special dinner – just as if, thought Amy sourly, she is in the way of arranging the meals when she knows it is I who manages the household when there isn't a man around to impress!

Dinner was held back an hour in the hope that Clarissa might arrive. They finally sat down, each one beginning to feel anxious. What was keeping the girl?

The new Earl of Greystone was a much-envied man. He had a stately home near Marlborough and fertile, rolling acres of land.

But the earl considered himself most unfortunate. He had returned from the wars in time for his father's funeral to find not only his stepmother, Angela, but her children, Bella, eighteen, Tom, seventeen, and Peregrine, aged eight, had been left to his care. He himself had had a strict and harsh upbringing, but his father, the late earl, had doted on his second wife and had let her spoil their children. The dowager countess, Angela, was, he sometimes felt, even more spoilt than her detestable offspring. She had been a vulgar woman when his father had married her and was now an extremely vulgar widow, given to throwing scenes when

15

she did not get her own way.

He had suggested that a season in Bath would be sufficient for Bella, but Angela had wept and sobbed until she had made him promise to open up the town house for the London Season and present Bella there.

The earl was thirty-two, but looked older. His black hair was streaked at the temples with lines of silver. His harsh, strong face had a brooding look and his pale-blue eyes were like winter ice. He was well over six feet tall. Angela told everyone who would listen that he was a tyrant and quite a few believed her and said that as the Earl of Greystone looked like Satan, then it must follow that he behaved as devilishly as his stepmother claimed.

He had had a flaming row with Tom that very day. His half-brother had demanded money to buy a new hunter. The earl had pointed out that the young man already had a fine hunter and Tom had pouted and claimed that a horse which Gully Banks, in Marlborough, had on offer, was as fine a beast as could be found going for a song outside Tattersall's. The 'song' turned out to be eight hundred pounds. The earl had said calmly he knew Gully Banks to be a villain. Tom had howled that the earl held the purse-strings so tight, it was a wonder they even had anything to eat. The result was Tom had been ordered to his room and told to stay there until further notice.

Dinner was a dismal meal. Angela liked country hours and so dinner was served at four. She said that poor Tom was so wretched he would do himself a mischief and then proceeded to sob noisily throughout the meal. Then young Peregrine enlivened the scene by letting off a firework in the dining room that blasted a hole in the plaster of the ceiling. Bella shrieked with laughter but Angela simply shrieked and shrieked as the earl cuffed Peregrine and sent *him* to his room.

The earl threw down his napkin and made his escape. He decided to look in on Tom and make sure that young man was not up to any mischief.

Tom's room was empty. A copy of a book entitled *Famous Highwaymen* lay face down on the floor, along with little bits of black velvet and a pair of scissors. The earl's lips tightened. He went straight to the gunroom, where his worst fears were resolved. A long box that had held two duelling pistols lay open and empty on the table in the middle of the gun room.

He changed out of the evening dress which

he always wore for dinner into his riding clothes, called for his horse, and set out into the night to rescue this infuriating half-brother who had obviously decided to turn highwayman.

The Honourable Clarissa Vevian was beginning to enjoy herself. The day had been quite dreadful, with Mama holding back the coach because Clarissa's new wardrobe was not ready and then deciding that Clarissa should spend two nights at posting-houses on the road. She would be late arriving in London, one whole day late, but the viscountess was sure the Tribbles would understand.

As soon as the coach rolled out of Bath, Clarissa took out a small damp face cloth that she had wrapped in oilskin and vigorously scrubbed every bit of white lead paint from her face and then threw the cloth out of the window.

'Miss Clarissa,' admonished her maid, Hubbard, sternly, 'you know my lady does not like you to go out in the world unpainted.'

'Well, Mama isn't here to see it,' said Clarissa cheerfully. And the fact that Mama would not be around to see anything for quite some time sent her spirits soaring.

Clarissa adored her dainty mother, but Lady Clarendon crushed Clarissa's spirits more than a less affectionate parent might have done. Lady Clarendon tried so hard to beautify her daughter, unfortunately choosing for her fashions that would have looked splendid on her own trim figure, but made her giantess of a daughter appear even more gauche. It was very lowering to the spirits, reflected Clarissa, to have a mother who was always so sadly disappointed in one. Now the maid, Hubbard, was fat and cross and dumpy and made Clarissa feel quite pretty in comparison. Of course these Tribbles might turn out to be fearfully elegant and might make her feel like a guy, but for the moment Clarissa was determined to enjoy what little liberty she had.

Her feet hurt, for Lady Clarendon had bought her daughter shoes too small for her in an attempt to make her large feet look smaller. Clarissa bent down and untied the ribbons and eased her feet out of them with a sigh and luxuriously wiggled her toes. Then she took a flat case out of her reticule, extracted a cheroot and a tinder-box and proceeded to try to light it.

'Miss Clarissa,' exclaimed Hubbard, 'don't you dare.'

'Do be quiet, Hubbard, I've always wanted to try one.'

Clarissa succeeded in lighting the cheroot. She drew in a lungful of smoke and then fell about the carriage coughing and gasping.

The carriage lurched to a halt.

'Stand and deliver!' called a voice from outside.

'Highwaymen!' screamed Hubbard. 'We'll be killed dead.'

'It can't be highwaymen. Not on this road,' said Clarissa.

Still holding the smouldering cheroot, she tugged at the strap and let down the glass and stuck her head out. It was a clear, starry night. There was a masked figure on top of a black horse, waving a pistol in a threatening way.

'Step down from that carriage,' called the highwayman, 'and bring your jewels and money with you or I shall shoot your coachman.'

'Oh, very well,' grumbled Clarissa. 'Find the jewel box, Hubbard. If we give this fellow what he wants, he may ride off and leave us unharmed.'

But the fat maid was rolling on the carriage floor, sobbing and screaming. Clarissa bent down and pulled the jewel box out from under the seat and, putting it under one arm but still holding the forgotten cheroot in her free hand, she stepped down from the carriage. The highwayman edged his horse close to her. 'Hand it over,' he growled.

Clarissa took a step forward, but she was in her stockinged feet, and one foot came down on a sharp piece of flint. She let out a yell and dropped the box and stumbled forward, the lighted end of her cheroot brushing against the horse's flanks. The horse reared up and threw the highwayman onto the road. He fell with a crash and lay still.

'You are not very good protection, are you?' said Clarissa to the two outriders, two grooms, and coachman. 'Bring me a lantern until I get a look at him.'

She tossed her cheroot into the carriage. The maid had tumbled out onto the road, where she was now sitting, sobbing dismally.

One of the grooms brought a lantern and Clarissa took it and bent over the still figure on the road. She knelt down and removed the black velvet mask.

'Why, 'tis only a boy!' she cried. She loosened his cravat. Tom had only been winded but thought it better to feign unconsciousness. 'I need water to bathe his temples,' said Clarissa. She looked at the side of the road and caught a faint gleam. She took out a large serviceable handkerchief and went over to the ditch, soaked the handkerchief and then placed it on Tom's brow. The 'highwayman' sat up with a roar. 'Eugh!' he cried. 'What a smell!' Clarissa sniffed her fingers and said in dismay, 'It must have been an open sewer. I am so sorry. For heaven's sake, Hubbard, stop wailing and get me the bottle of drinking water. Why did I forget that?'

'No, no,' said Tom. 'Don't do anything more to me, I beg. I am frightfully sorry. A joke, ma'am.'

'In poor taste,' said Clarissa severely.

The grooms, coachman, and outriders had gathered around Clarissa and the fallen Tom in a circle. Hubbard pushed her way through them and looked down at Tom. In the light of the lantern, she saw a very young man with a mop of fair curls and a face that might have been handsome had it not been smeared with Clarissa's offering from the sewer.

'Pooh! What a stink,' said Clarissa. 'Fetch me the cologne, Hubbard.'

Clarissa's cheroot, which she had tossed into the carriage, had fallen onto the open pages of a book which she had been reading, and it had proceeded to burn merrily while she was administering to Tom. The flames had travelled to the maid's cane basket and taken greedy hold.

As Hubbard approached the carriage, a long tongue of flame shot out of the window. 'Fire!' she screamed.

Swearing horribly, the coachman and grooms ran to unhitch the plunging and frightened horses and lead them to safety. Tom scrambled to his feet. His own horse had run off. But before he got a few yards down the road, a ball whizzed over his head. He stood stock-still, shaking with fright. Clarissa had seized his fallen pistol and had fired over his retreating figure.

He thought she looked like a she-devil when he slowly turned around with his hands raised and saw her walking towards him, the smoking pistol in her hand and the red glare of the burning carriage behind her.

He threw back his head and screamed, 'Help. Oh, help me!'

And then Clarissa heard the urgent thud of hooves coming along the road towards them at a great rate. 'Your accomplice, no doubt,' she said bitterly.

The Earl of Greystone rode towards that incredible scene. A carriage was burning brightly and in its lurid flames he saw his half-brother cringing before a tall female who was standing in her stockinged feet and holding a pistol.

He came to a halt and dismounted. 'Are you all right, Tom?' he asked.

'Keep her away from me,' cried Tom, and burst into tears.

The earl faced Clarissa. 'What has been going on, ma'am?'

Clarissa forgot to stoop. After all, she did not need to when faced with such a giant as this. 'This fellow held up my coach,' she said.

'Tom, stop blubbing,' snapped the earl. He turned back to Clarissa. 'And did he also set your coach on fire?'

'No, sir,' said Clarissa. 'I did that. It was the cheroot I was smoking, don't you see?'

'Take me home, Crispin,' wailed Tom, clutching at the earl's sleeve. The earl shook himself free. 'Faugh! What is that sickening smell?'

'I was trying to bathe his forehead,' said Clarissa patiently. 'You see, he ordered me down from the coach and asked for my jewels, and I was going to give them to him, you know, but I forgot about the cheroot and it burned his horse's side and his horse threw him and I soaked my handkerchief in that ditch over there and put it to his forehead, but that ditch, sir, is an open sewer. Hence the smell. I gather you are not highwaymen?'

'No, ma'am, I am Greystone. And you...?'

'Miss Vevian, Clarissa Vevian.'

'Miss Vevian, what can I say? This is dreadful. I pray you, leave this young whippersnapper to me and don't turn him over to the authorities. I will repair any damage to your property and give you a sum of money to cover your losses.'

'That's handsome of you,' said Clarissa, 'considering it was I who set the coach on fire. All my fine gowns are quite destroyed,' she said cheerfully, thinking of all those frilly, fussy dresses going up in smoke, not to mention all those cramping and crippling pairs of shoes.

'I suggest you ride back with me to my home and let the others find their own way there.'

'Very well,' said Clarissa. 'We are not totally ruined, for the jewels are still there and the money was in sovereigns. Pray give instructions to my servants.'

He strode off to talk to Clarissa's coachman. Tom sniffed dismally at Clarissa's elbow.

'Oh, you're still here,' said Clarissa crossly. "What an idiot you are!'

'It's all Crispin's fault,' said Tom. 'I asked

him for money for a new hunter and he wouldn't give it to me. He's a miser!'

'Was that his fine horse you were riding?'

'No, it was my own,' said Tom sulkily.

'But because you couldn't get your own way, you decided to turn highwayman and rob some defenceless person. Fie, for shame! My coachman could have shot you, had he had his wits about him. You are a silly little schoolboy.'

'I'll get even with you for this,' muttered Tom.

The earl strode back to them. 'Tom, help the maid mount one of the carriage horses and lead her home. Miss Vevian, let me help you mount.'

'I am quite capable of mounting myself,' said Clarissa, suddenly nervous of him. She put a stockinged foot in the stirrup and mounted with such energy that she went clean over the other side. Her bonnet fell off and her red hair, which was very long, tumbled down to her waist.

'Miss Vevian,' said the earl, picking her up. 'Do allow me to assist you.'

Despite Clarissa's height, he threw her up easily into the saddle and then mounted behind her and put a strong arm about her waist. He leaned forward and murmured in her ear, 'You do still smell awfully of that sewer,' before spurring his horse.

So much for romance, thought Clarissa tearfully as they rode through the starry night. Here she was, just like a heroine in a book, flying through the night with this man's hand at her waist and all he could murmur in her ear was that she smelled awful.

But she had no fear of him or that he might turn out to be a robber after all. He rode up the long drive of an estate and after a mile or so they came to a huge building. The lantern over the step was shining down on a pair of women who were waiting anxiously.

Clarissa looked down on them and her heart sank. They were just the sort of ladies who always made her feel clumsy. The older one was still pretty in a faded way with clusters of brown curls confined with a gold fillet over her brow. The younger had golden hair and delicate features.

The earl dismounted and helped Clarissa down. 'Where is Tom?' demanded Angela.

'Tom will be here presently,' said the earl. 'This is Miss Vevian, whose coach he tried to rob. Miss Vevian, my stepmother, the Dowager Countess of Greystone, and my half-sister, Lady Bella.'

'You must be mistaken. Tom would never do such a thing,' exclaimed Angela.

'He did, he has, and you must pray that Miss Vevian here does not turn him over to the nearest magistrate.'

To Clarissa's dismay, Angela threw herself at her feet and cried, 'Oh, spare my boy.'

'Please take Miss Vevian indoors and find her clean clothes and water to wash and bring her to the saloon and we will discuss the matter,' said the earl testily.

But it was only with great difficulty that Angela could be persuaded to behave herself. Clarissa was glad Angela was led off by Bella and she herself was turned over to the care of an efficient housekeeper.

It transpired that the earl's mother had been as tall as Clarissa and that her feet had been as large. Although she had been dead for many years now, her clothes were still stored in the attics. A gown of dark-green velvet was found for Clarissa and a pair of shoes with high red heels. Clarissa brushed her own hair and twisted it into a knot on the top of her head. She made her way to the saloon guided by a footman, feeling she looked like a guy.

The footman opened the door for her and

she walked in. There was no one in the room but the earl, who was standing by the fireplace.

There was a little silence while the pair surveyed each other. Clarissa saw that the earl was indeed much taller than she was herself. He was handsome but formidable with his thick black hair, strong face, and pale, cold eyes. The earl saw a slim girl in a green velvet gown with thick masses of fiery-red hair, a rather sweet face dusted with freckles, and wide-spaced grey eyes; Clarissa noticed with surprise that the earl was looking at her with the same expression in his eyes which certain elderly gentleman had when they paid court to her mother – warmth and admiration. She felt quite breathless with surprise.

'Come and sit down by the fire, Miss Vevian,' said the earl, 'and warm yourself. I do apologize for that wretched boy. Do say you forgive us.'

'Yes, I do forgive you,' said Clarissa. 'It must be very taxing for you to have such a difficult charge. I have heard of you, my lord. Your father died recently and Tom is your half-brother.'

'I wish I knew what to do with the boy. He is sadly spoilt. We are going to London for the Season and I shudder to think what scrapes he will get into.'

'Then don't take him,' said Clarissa, stretching her hands gratefully to the blaze.

'I can hardly leave him here on his own.'

'No, but if you hired an excellent tutor, you could send him off on the Grand Tour. The prospect of travel would excite him. You would not have the responsibility of him for some time. Have you any other half-brothers?'

'Peregrine, aged eight. Another spoilt brat.'

'But just the right age to go to school,' said Clarissa. 'Send him to Eton.'

'My dear Miss Vevian, he would never go, and his mother and Bella would scream the house down.'

'Then tell both of them that you have no intention of wasting good money in sending the boy to school,' said Clarissa. 'You will find it will work like magic. People are very contrary-minded, or so I have observed.'

'Do you usually deal with other people's troubles in this practical manner?'

'No, I grew up, you see, as soon as I left home, which was today.'

He smiled. 'And can you not be grown up at home?'

'No, my dear mama still thinks of me as a

little girl and I would do anything to please her,' said Clarissa sadly.

'And why were you on the road to London, and should I send a messenger on ahead to explain the delay?'

'That would be very kind,' said Clarissa. 'If you could advise the Misses Tribble of Holles Street that I have broken my journey, I would be most grateful.'

'The Tribbles? The professional chaperones? Is that where you are bound? Why?'

'I did not "take" in Bath,' said Clarissa, blushing painfully. 'I am a trifle awkward.'

'You mean you usually set fire to carriages and bathe foreheads with handkerchiefs dipped in a sewer?'

'Something like that,' said Clarissa wretchedly. The earl felt laughter bubbling up inside him. He had not felt so amused and happy in a long while.

He held out a case. 'Have a cheroot, Miss Vevian.'

Clarissa shuddered and waved the case away. 'No, no. I do not smoke them. I was only trying one to be, well, bold and independent and free.'

'I see,' he said gently. 'Here is the punch-bowl, Miss Vevian. A glass will restore you.'

The servant set a tray with the ingredients

for punch on a table beside the earl. Clarissa watched him enviously as he deftly mixed the ingredients. Nothing spilled and nothing dropped.

He handed her a glass. Clarissa settled back in her comfortable chair. The fire crackled, the clocks ticked, and the wind howled in the chimney. She wished she could go on sitting here with this man, who made her feel quite small and feminine.

'Why do you not stay here for a little as my guest?' he said as if reading her thoughts. 'I could write to your parents.'

'It would not answer,' said Clarissa sadly. 'You see, Mama and Papa would probably come and stay as well and Mama would make me wear small tight shoes again and small tight flounced dresses and of course I would wear them to please her. But if I go to London, I can choose the type of clothes I would really like to wear – clothes like this.'

'A trifle old-fashioned. That gown was my mother's.'

'But she must have been big like me,' said Clarissa, 'and she dressed to suit her size. This gown may be old-fashioned, but it was a modish gown in its day.'

'It becomes you, Miss Vevian.'

Clarissa gave him a blinding smile.

'In fact, you may keep it and anything else you are provided with for your journey.'

'But your mother's clothes...'

'She would have been delighted could she have known they were being put to good use. She was a kind and charming lady. My father, alas, was a brute and a tyrant. She did not have a happy life.'

'If he was a brute and a tyrant, how is it that Tom and Peregrine and Lady Bella are so spoilt?'

'He doted on Angela. She was considerably younger than he. There was a vulgar streak in my father. Angela is vulgar underneath that clinging and pretty façade. Dear me. Pretend I never said that. Do people always converse so openly with you?'

'No,' said Clarissa. 'My height intimidates them and then I am very shy.'

'You do not seem in the least shy to me.'

'That is because of the circumstances. We are here by chance, you see I am not being paraded in front of you in the hope you might marry me. I do not need to *try*. Do you know what I mean?'

'Yes,' he said, taking her glass and refilling it. 'I know what you mean.' He privately thought Lady Clarendon was, however unwittingly, guilty of being cruel and callous.

'In fact, I often wish I were a man.' Clarissa moved her arm in an expansive gesture and a little wave of punch slopped onto the green gown. She let out a wail of dismay.

He took out his handkerchief and dabbed at the stain on her bust. 'No, don't!' cried Clarissa, pushing his hand away.

'I am merely trying to take the stain out, Miss Vevian.'

Clarissa miserably shook her head. Her whole body felt on fire. 'I think I shall retire, my lord.'

'Of course,' he said quickly. 'You must be tired after your adventures.' He rang the bell and ordered a footman to show Clarissa to her room.

Clarissa found a nightgown laid out for her. She undressed and washed herself again in case any of that awful sewer smell should still prove to be lingering about and brushed out her hair and then remembered her maid, Hubbard, and went in search of her. She should have called for a servant and asked the way, but she was clad only in her night-gown and wanted to have a talk in private with Hubbard. She judged the maid would have been put in one of the rooms on the upper floor. She pushed open several doors until she found the right one.

Hubbard was sitting up in bed, reading a Bible.

'I was told you were downstairs, miss,' said Hubbard, 'so I asked that housekeeper to fetch me the Bible to show this household we are God-fearing folk.'

'There was no need,' said Clarissa. 'Lord Greystone is all that is respectable.'

'Lets his half-brother go around holding up coaches? That's not respectable.'

'It is very difficult to explain, Hubbard. We shall set out tomorrow. Lord Greystone is sending a letter to the Tribbles to explain the delay in our arrival, which is something Mama should have done in the first place, for we were almost a day late in leaving Bath.'

'My nerves is shattered, miss,' said Hubbard huffily. 'Don't seem right it should be all hushed up.'

'Hubbard, you will not say one word. I am sure Master Tom will be punished. Lord Greystone has promised to pay for a new carriage and for all the clothes we have lost. Now, go to sleep.'

'Don't be getting into any mischief, miss. I had better see you to your room. You shouldn't ought to be wandering about in your night-rail, and with his lordship not wed.'

'We are adequately chaperoned by his step-mother, and you know it. Good night, Hubbard.'

Clarissa left the maid's room and stifled a yawn. She was suddenly extremely weary. She could not remember ever being so tired. She wandered downstairs and then stood irresolute. Which was her room? She turned this way and that and finally made her way along a passage and gently opened a door. Bella was sitting up in bed reading.

'What do *you* want?' she asked rudely.

'I have lost my bedroom,' said Clarissa.

Bella surveyed her for a few moments and then smiled. She climbed out of bed. 'I will show you where it is. Follow me.'

Back into the passage, which was lit by an oil lamp, along two more passages. Bella stopped outside a door. 'In there,' she said. 'That's your room.'

Clarissa curtsied awkwardly, feeling once more tall and gauche beside the dainty creature that was Bella. 'Thank you,' she said softly. 'Good night.'

'Pleasant dreams,' said Bella with a little laugh.

Clarissa went into the room and shut the door. A fire was glowing in the hearth. She walked to the large bed and pulled back the bed-curtains. Strange that the bed seemed to have grown much larger than when she had last seen it. She climbed in and fell asleep as soon as her head hit the pillow.

The Earl of Greystone went into his room and took off his clothes, thinking hard of what Clarissa had said as he did so. It would be wonderful if he could get Peregrine off to school and Tom off on the Grand Tour. Then he would only have Bella and Angela to cope with. Bella was very pretty and would no doubt be married and off his hands before the Season was over. If only Angela would marry again. That would solve all his problems. He filled the basin on the toilet table with rose-scented water and splashed himself all over and scrubbed himself down with a towel.

He wondered whether to light the candles and read for a little but decided against it. He climbed into bed and stretched his naked body out under the sheets.

Then he heard a soft rhythmic breathing close to his ear. He stretched out and fumbled with the tinder-box and lit the candle in its flat stick beside the bed and held it up. Red hair cascaded over the pillow beside him. He could just see the tip of Miss Clarissa Vevian's small nose.

And to think he had liked her immensely! He was rich, he was a bachelor, and this girl who was so unmarriageable that she had been sent away to the Tribbles was trying to entrap him.

He walked round to her side of the bed and jerked back the bed-curtains and shook her roughly by the shoulder.

Clarissa's eyes opened. They ranged up the long length of his naked body and she opened her mouth to scream. He clamped a hand over it. 'No, you will not ruin my reputation and make me marry you, you minx,' he said.

Clarissa struggled and fought and he saw in the candlelight that her eyes were wide with terror. He leaned down and said quietly, 'I will take my hand away if you promise not to scream.' Clarissa nodded and he took his hand from her mouth.

'What are you doing in my bed?' he hissed.

'I lost my way to my room,' whispered Clarissa fiercely. 'I asked Lady Bella where it was and she showed me in here.'

'Damn Bella,' he said, sitting down on the bed. 'I am very sorry, Miss Vevian. I thought you were trying to compromise me.'

'And I thought you were going to rape me,' said Clarissa. He picked up the coverlet and draped it about him and then crossed the room and took his dressing gown down from a hook at the back of the door and put it on.

'The sooner you leave for London, the better,' he said ruefully. 'A pox on my wretched relatives. Do not say a word of this, Miss Vevian. We will let Bella think you found out her trick. Come along, I will take you to your room.'

Clarissa began to laugh. 'What an adventure,' she said. 'You looked exactly like the wicked seducer in a book, except they are never so indecent in the illustrations.'

He held open the door. 'Come. You are a brave and most forgiving lady.'

He led her back the way she had come to a door beside Bella's bedchamber. 'In here,' he said.

'Thank you,' said Clarissa, suddenly shy.

He raised her hand to his lips and kissed it.

'Good night and sleep well, my beautiful Miss Vevian.'

But Clarissa was so radiantly happy that it was quite an hour before she got to sleep.

She found the leave-taking the next day very hard. Lord Greystone looked tall and elegant and remote. She wanted to ask him if she would see him again, but he simply shook her by the hand and repeated he would make good any losses she had suffered.

'Thank you, my lord,' she said sadly. She followed Hubbard into the earl's travelling coach and sat down. He rapped on the glass and she let it down.

'Tell the Tribbles I shall be calling,' he said. 'We must settle our accounts.'

'Oh, yes ... yes, of course,' said Clarissa, suddenly happy.

The carriage rolled off. Lord Greystone raised his hand in farewell and went into the house with a smile on his lips.

'Do you see that smile?' Angela asked her daughter. 'He must not marry. The money must come to you and Perry and poor Tom.'

'She couldn't find her room last night,' said Bella, 'so I showed her into his and said it was hers. Perhaps they had a splendid night together.'

'You little fool, Bella. Why did you do such a thing?'

'I thought it would give them both a fright ... create a bit of scandal,' said Bella with a shrug. 'Do not worry, Mama, we are going to London ourselves and will make sure they never get together again.'

In the carriage, Clarissa luxuriously wiggled her toes inside a pair of smart and large-enough half-boots, courtesy of the late countess's wardrobe, as was the fur cloak wrapped about her and the elegant hat on her head. She felt as if all the constrictions of the past, both physical and mental, were slipping away.

She put her head out of the carriage window. A pale shaft of sunlight lit up the road ahead.

Clarissa sat down again. 'I have left myself behind,' she said happily.

'You're talking nonsense, miss,' grumbled Hubbard, 'and what would your poor mama say if she could see you without a lick of paint on your face and all them freckles.'

A shadow crossed Clarissa's face. But then she brightened. He had called her beautiful, and no one was going to take that wonderful moment away from her.

2

Napoleon hoped that all the world would fall beneath his sway;
He failed in his ambition, and where is he today?
Neither the Nations of the East nor the Nations of the West
Have thought the thing Napoleon thought was to their interest.

An Unknown Lieutenant-Colonel

Before Clarissa and Hubbard could reach the posting-house where they were to spend the night, the carriage was stopped. They heard the sounds of a great commotion and a voice ordering the coachman to halt.

The maid turned a muddy colour. 'Not highwaymen again,' she bleated.

Clarissa put her head out of the carriage window and then turned round and said over her shoulder, 'Not highwaymen, Hubbard. Redcoats. I wonder what they want. I am too tired to fuss. We'll wait and see.' She sat down again and waited patiently.

43

The carriage door was opened and a colonel bowed low and said, 'I have instructions to search all carriages on this road, ma'am.'

'Why?' asked Clarissa.

'Valuable government papers have been stolen, ma'am.'

'We are not French spies,' said Clarissa, 'and we are tired and hungry. Please do not take very long.'

He saluted and disappeared from view.

Soon both women could hear the trunks being unstrapped from the back. There was very little luggage, such as there was having come from Lord Greystone – dresses and pelisses, hats and shoes for Clarissa, and uniforms for the servants.

The colonel reappeared. 'Anything in the carriage, ladies?'

'Just the jewel box and the lace box,' said Clarissa. 'Stop trembling and whimpering, Hubbard, and help me get them out from under the seat.'

Two still smoke-blackened cases were produced. The colonel examined the contents in a perfunctory way as if having already made up his mind that he was wasting his time with this young girl and her maid.

'Thank you,' he said. 'I am most sorry to have inconvenienced you. You may drive on.'

'Surely we no longer need to worry about French spies with that monster locked up on the island,' said Clarissa.

'Napoleon has escaped,' said the colonel grimly.

He slammed the carriage door and called to the coachman and the carriage lurched forward once more.

'Oh, he has escaped,' cried Hubbard. 'We will all be murdered in our beds, or worse!'

'Wretched man,' said Clarissa, meaning Napoleon. 'Now we shall be at war again and everything will cost the earth. Still, the Duke of Wellington will soon rout him.'

In an hour's time, they reached The Bell, a prosperous posting-house. The earl's servant, the one who had ridden ahead to the Tribbles with the news of Clarissa's delay, had bespoken a room for them, but the landlord regretted they could not have a private parlour.

'No matter,' said Clarissa, stifling a yawn. 'We will eat in the public dining room.'

The posting-house was full of people, fashionable people. Clarissa's heart sank. Then she remembered the earl had called her beautiful and she straightened her shoulders as she walked down to the dining room after having washed and changed. Clothes were such a help. She was wearing another of the earl's mother's gowns. It was of old gold silk with a low square neckline and long tight sleeves, rather like a gown in a Renaissance painting. Clarissa was wearing a simple necklace of seed pearls because her finer jewellery was all smoke-blackened and would have to be cleaned.

Deaf to her maid's protests, Clarissa ordered champagne, a drink she had longed to try but had never been allowed to touch before, her mother considering it too exotic and heady a drink for a young miss. Clarissa sober was clumsy enough. Clarissa drunk could be downright dangerous.

Hubbard was determined to drink as much of the champagne herself as she could in order to prevent disaster. The maid was being paid high wages – danger money – to see that Clarissa did not set rooms on fire or fall down the stairs.

They had a clear soup followed by *filet de sole à la Orly* and finished the champagne. Clarissa ordered a bottle of Médoc, a St Peray, to go with the raised pie, the saddle of mutton, and the roast pigeons. Hubbard had hardly ever drunk anything stronger than lemonade before. Her eyes closed and she began to snore. Clarissa looked at her crossly. 'Pig,' she muttered. 'You can just stay there until I have finished this excellent meal.'

By the time the floating-island pudding was served – Clarissa decided to eat Hubbard's as well as her own – people were beginning to leave the dining room. Slowly the long tables emptied.

Comforted by wine and food, Clarissa relaxed. No one was looking at her and she had not spilled a drop or stained the tablecloth. Clumsy Clarissa no more!

She would have been surprised to learn that she had, in fact, attracted a great deal of interest. A Clarissa with her flaming hair covered by a turban, her shoulders stooped, and her face whitened with blanc, crouched by the side of her decorative parents, was one thing, but this new Clarissa, with flaming red hair piled high on her head, in a gold silk gown that revealed the excellence of her bosom, was another matter.

Mr Roger Epsom nursed his brandy glass and studied Clarissa. What a magnificent giantess, he thought, and – gad! – what shoulders. He was feeling elated, not with wine or with the sight of Clarissa, but because of his recent narrow escape. In his bosom reposed a packet of government papers that he was taking to France, where he would be suitably rewarded for them. He had been approached by a certain gentleman when his debts were at their highest. This gentleman had pointed out that General Chomley's daughter seemed very taken with Mr Epsom. Mr Epsom had laughed and said that he was not interested in marrying or courting any female. The gentleman had said that if Mr Epsom could inveigle himself into the household and find where the general kept certain papers, take them, and then journey with them to an address in Paris, he would be rewarded with a fortune.

Mr Epsom had been paid quite a large sum in advance. He did not feel like a traitor. He felt sure the Duke of Wellington would trounce the French once more whatever he did. It was an adventure and one he enjoyed. He had found that the papers were kept in a safe in the general's office and had taken a note of the make. Then he had gone to safe makers in Pall Mall and had said he was interested in purchasing one of the same type. While they were demonstrating how the lock worked, he had managed to slip the keys into his pocket. He had taken the keys to a certain address in Whitechapel and had had them copied. Then he had returned the original keys to the safe maker with many apologies.

A ball held at the general's house was all the opportunity he needed. He slipped away from the guests and into the general's office. Although the makers of the safe had boasted that each of their products was supplied with an individual lock, Mr Epsom had, quite rightly, not believed them. They were inferior locksmiths, not of the calibre of, say, Chubb. The safe had opened easily. He'd taken the papers giving the details of the strength of the British troops on the Continent, sealed them up in the oilskin packet, and gone back and joined the dancing.

He had not expected their loss to be discovered so quickly and was thankful now he had taken the precaution of carrying the papers in an oilskin packet under his shirt. All roads and inns and posting-houses were being searched and every volunteer regiment and every parish constable had been pressed into the hunt.

He was sure they would not have a description of him – not yet. He had been one of many young men who had called at the general's home to pay court to his pretty daughter, Miss Kitty, although Mr Epsom had only been there in the first place because Miss Kitty was the fashion.

He and his carriage had been searched.

He could relax.

Clarissa was now drinking brandy. She would have a head like the devil in the morning, he thought. And then he heard a commotion outside in the yard. He rose slowly and went to the window.

Redcoats!

Swarms and swarms of them.

Damn. He had chosen the one posting-house that had surely not yet been searched.

He turned around. Clarissa was trying to wake her maid.

He thought quickly. 'May I be of assistance, ma'am?' he said, going up to her. Clarissa looked down at him. She saw a pleasant, well-dressed young man with a face like an amiable rabbit. His teeth were slightly protruding and his eyes were prominent.

'If you would be so kind, sir,' she said. 'Do wake up, Hubbard.'

Hubbard at last woke and looked about vaguely. 'Whassmatter?' she said.

'You fell asleep,' said Clarissa crossly.

'Perhaps if you will give me the key to her room,' said Mr Epsom, 'I could go ahead of you and open the door.'

'She is sharing my room, the Jupiter Room to the left of the first landing,' said Clarissa. 'Here is the key. I shall help her up the stairs.'

50

Mr Epsom sauntered out, but once outside the door, he darted up the stairs as fast as he could. He opened the door to Clarissa's room and looked wildly about. Down below, he could hear the commotion as the soldiers began their search. He saw Clarissa's jewel box and opened it up. He removed the trays of rings from the top, pulled out brooches and necklaces, opened his waistcoat and shirt and took out the oilskin packet of papers and placed it in the bottom, and hurriedly put everything back inside again. He slammed down the lid and then went out to pretend he was nothing more than an innocent helper of ladies in distress.

Clarissa was halfway up the stairs, holding a semi-conscious Hubbard and complaining, 'You wretched fool. How could this happen? You only had half a bottle of champagne.' Hubbard recovered consciousness again. 'God bless His Majesty!' she roared.

'Let me help you,' said Mr Epsom, coming down the stairs. 'Here is your key.'

Hubbard had gone to sleep again. Clarissa shoved her body over the banisters, where it hung like a sack, and held out her hand for the key.

'Thank you, sir,' she said. 'If I take one side and you the other, we might be able to 'get her to bed.'

'Gladly,' he said with a smile.

Then Clarissa stopped and stood rigid, her eyes staring out into space. Mr Epsom looked at her anxiously. Foxed as well as her maid, he thought.

But Clarissa had noticed Mr Epsom's gloves when he handed her the key. Those lavender gloves were streaked with black marks. They had not had a mark on them when he left the dining room. She had noticed them particularly, thinking them a very pretty shade of lavender.

She turned and looked down at him, her eyes blazing. 'You have been in my jewel box,' she said.

Mr Epsom turned pale. 'Bless me, ma'am. As if I would. Is this the way you repay kindness – with mad accusations? Come, let me help you with your maid.'

'Get away from me! Thief!' said Clarissa, lashing out. She struck him a blow across the chest and, with a wail of surprise, he somersaulted down the stairs. There was a sickening crash as he hit the floor and then he lay still.

What have I done? thought Clarissa.

She ran down the stairs and searched frantically through Mr Epsom's pockets. Not a single jewel. She leaned over him. He was breathing, but she did not know how long he would continue to breathe. The door opened and the colonel who had searched her carnage stood there, with some of his men behind him.

'What has happened, ma'am?' he asked, looking from Hubbard, slouched over the banisters, to Mr Epsom's still form.

Clarissa's one thought was that if she had killed this man, she would hang. If he had been trying to steal from her, then *he* would hang. And she could not bear either of those prospects. Despite the vast crowds which still turned out to see a public hanging, many malefactors still went scot-free, since a surprising number of people could not bring themselves to bear witness against them and so be the cause of their death. Hanging, instead of being a deterrent to the criminal, was rapidly becoming an impediment to the course of justice.

'He was trying to help me get my maid to bed,' said Clarissa, 'and he fell and struck his head. Is he dead?'

The colonel knelt down by the fallen Mr Epsom. 'No, ma'am, just unconscious. We'll call the physician. I remember you, ma'am; we have already searched your bags and carriage.' He called over his shoulder. 'Here, two of you, carry this lady's maid up to her room.'

Hubbard was lifted by two redcoats and carried up the stairs and dumped on the trucklebed in the corner of Clarissa's room.

Clarissa waited until they had left and then she locked the door. She went to her jewel case and opened it. She saw at once that he had been in it. The rings were scattered about instead of being neatly arranged in their compartments. She lifted out the trays. Everything seemed to be there. To be sure, she counted everything carefully; so intent on counting the pieces of jewellery was she that she did not notice the flat black oilskin packet at the bottom of the box.

She put all the jewellery back in and slammed down the lid, washed her hands, and then looked down at her sleeping maid.

She can just sleep with her clothes on, thought Clarissa, for she is too heavy to undress.

Clarissa had a disturbed night. She was awakened by the groans of Hubbard and had to minister to her. She did not feel very well herself. Her head was hot and the bed showed an alarming tendency to run around the room every time she tried to lay her head on the pillow.

At least I know something, thought Clarissa dismally. Lots of drink is no fun at all. We must leave very early or that poor man will awake and try to charge me with assault. But, of course, he is a thief, so he will probably keep quiet. I suppose I should tell the authorities, for if he is not checked then he will try to thieve again. But that would mean a hanging and I could not bear that.

By seven in the morning, Clarissa had decided she'd had enough of the posting-house and its adventures. She went downstairs to order the carriage to be brought round and to pay her shot. She was ridiculously happy when the landlord told her it had already been paid by the Earl of Greystone. A small courtesy but one which gladdened Clarissa's heart.

Mr Haddon called on the Tribbles two days after he had had dinner with them. To his dismay, there was no sign and no word of the Honourable Clarissa Vevian.

'What if Georgina changed her mind?' wailed Effy, too anguished to flirt. 'What will we do?'

'I fear you must advertise again,' said Mr Haddon. 'But give it a few more days. The roads can be treacherous. There may have been a storm. Then there has been a great fuss over some missing government papers, and all the inns and posting-houses and carriages are being searched. Say the thief was discovered to be in some town. The army might seal off that town and make a house-to-house search, and if that town was on the road from Bath, then this Miss Clarissa would be compelled to stay there.'

'I know something awful has happened,' said Effy. 'Now I come to think of it, dear Georgina was always feckless and scatter-brained and flighty. She has no doubt forgotten our existence. Or what if she did not know of the wild events that have taken place here, and someone has now told her, and she has decided we are not fit chaperones for Clarissa?'

'Oh, stop!' said Amy, clutching her head. 'We've had everything in this house arranged and rearranged and we've flown into a dither every time a carriage passes in the street below. I'm weary. I think I don't like Clarissa or her family. We're probably better off without her. She's probably got a face on her like a pig's arse.'

'Miss Amy! Really!' admonished Mr Haddon, showing that he, too, was upset at the non-arrival of Clarissa, for usually he let Amy's vulgarities of speech pass without comment, knowing that Amy had been brought up in an age when coarseness was fashionable.

Amy blushed. 'Sorry,' she mumbled.

A knock sounded on the door downstairs. 'Don't leap about, Effy,' said Amy. 'It's probably a cheeky hawker, too lazy to go down the area steps.'

'No, no,' fluttered Effy. 'I am sure it is something about Clarissa.'

She ran out. Amy tried to change the subject. 'How is your friend from India getting along, Mr Haddon?'

'Mr Randolph? Very well. He, too, finds London strange after India. I helped him to find lodgings yesterday. It is pleasant to have a companion of like interests.'

Amy felt jealous of this Mr Randolph. Now, perhaps, Mr Haddon would not call on them so much.

Effy came back into the room, looking flushed and happy. 'It is a letter from the Earl of Greystone,' she said.

'And of what use is that?' growled Amy.

'Listen! He writes to say that Miss Clarissa Vevian had an accident to her carriage and will be delayed in arriving. He says – and this is most mysterious – that he holds himself responsible for the ruin of her carriage and loss of her baggage and will be calling on us before the end of the month to discuss payment. Well! Greystone ... Greystone...' Effy ran to the desk in the corner and took out her list of 'eligibles'. 'Ah, here he is. I knew I had heard the name recently. But it is in the 'Not Likely' column. He has recently inherited the title, lives near Marlborough, unwed, rich, but has not been seen in London yet. Do you think...?'

'No, I don't think,' said Amy. 'Still, I'm glad the girl is still on her way here. Does this Greystone give any idea when she might reach London?'

'He mentions she was staying a night with them. Let me see, she would need to break her journey again. With any luck, she should be here by late afternoon.'

Amy looked about her wearily. 'Everything's been done for her arrival that can be done. We can't hire any tutors until we find out her deficiences. Oh, Lor'. I wish we didn't have to have her.'

Amy was upset and bad tempered. She had a nagging ache in the small of her back and everything seemed to irritate her these days. Mr Haddon rose to take his leave. 'Oh,

I had forgot,' he said. 'A most momentous piece of news. Napoleon has escaped.'

'And Queen Anne's dead,' said Amy rudely. 'We heard that yesterday.

Mr Haddon's thin face flushed slightly. He looked down at Amy, who had not risen to curtsy goodbye to him but was still slouched in an armchair.

'I do not know what is wrong, Miss Amy,' said Mr Haddon severely. 'But of late, you have been snapping my head off. I thought we were friends. If I have done anything to offend you, please tell me.'

'Oh, no!' Amy shot to her feet and sent her chair flying. 'Dear Mr Haddon. I am a bear! A veritable bear! Pray forgive me. I would not have you cross with me for anything in the world.'

Her eyes were shining with tears and her face was a picture of distress.

Mr Haddon bent and kissed her hand and then smiled into her eyes. 'That's better,' he said softly. Amy looked at him in a dazed way and then slowly lifted the hand he had kissed to her bosom.

'Humph!' said Effy Tribble to no one in particular and threw a log on the fire with unnecessary force.

Mr Epsom recovered consciousness and opened his eyes to find a physician bending over him.

'What happened?' he asked.

'You had a fall down the stairs and banged your head,' said the physician. 'I have bled you and told the landlord to let you lie here quietly for a few days until your strength returns.'

'Thank you,' said Mr Epsom weakly. He furrowed his brow. 'Oh, I remember, tall girl. Helped her get her drunk maid up the stairs to ... her ... room...' His voice trailed away as memory came flooding back. The papers!

'I must get up!' He tried to leap out of bed, but the room whirled about him.

'Now, now, sir,' said the physician, pressing him back against the pillows. 'You will do yourself a mischief.'

Mr Epsom closed his eyes and breathed deeply. Then he opened them again and said, 'Please ask the tall lady with the red hair to step along and see me. She is a guest here. Don't know her name but should be easy to find. Gigantic female.'

'Do you think that wise? I–'

'Get her,' said Mr Epsom savagely.

He closed his eyes again and waited. But it

was the landlord who reappeared after what seemed an age.

'Beg pardon, Mr Epsom, sir,' he said, 'but the lady you was asking about left early this morning.'

Mr Epsom groaned. Then he asked, 'Who was she?'

The landlord scratched his wig. 'Don't rightly know, sir. The room was ordered and paid for by the Earl of Greystone, so I suppose the young lady must have been a member of his family.'

There came a light knock at the door and then a voice Mr Epsom knew only too well demanded, 'I hear my dear friend, Mr Epsom, is ill. Leave us, landlord. We wish to be private.'

The landlord bowed low before the finely dressed visitor.

The visitor waited until the landlord had left and then turned the key in the lock. He strolled up to the bed and said in a silky voice, 'Sorry to see you in such a coil. The ague?'

'No, was pushed down the stairs and knocked unconscious. Damned physician bled me while I was out and I'm as weak as a kitten.'

'Before I find out who it was who attacked

you, may I know whether you have the papers safe?'

'They're gone,' whispered Mr Epsom.

The visitor drew a pistol from his pocket and levelled it at Mr Epsom's head. 'Any more last words?' he asked pleasantly.

'No! Spare me. All may not be yet lost. Listen! You must listen. The soldiers were here last night searching the place. I was at my wit's end. I offered to help a red-haired female in the dining room who was having trouble with her tipsy maid. I asked her for the key to her room and volunteered to go ahead and open the door for her. She gave me the key. I ran up and hid the papers in the bottom of the jewel box, meaning to retrieve them later. We were on the stairs when this red-haired giantess suddenly stares at my gloves and accuses me of having been at her jewellery. I tried to protest and she struck me and that's the last I know. She is of Greystone's family. The papers can be retrieved before she ever finds them.'

'I think, my friend, I had better help you out of here in case the militia return. She may have discovered them already. She obviously fears she might have killed you, for she has not reported you as a thief. What was it about your gloves that alerted her?'

'I don't know. They must be with my clothes. Lavender pair. Kid.'

The visitor walked across the room and searched until he found the gloves. 'They're smeared with black, as if they'd touched something which had been in a fire,' he said. 'Either she smeared her jewels with the stuff or they have been in a fire. In any case, the sooner we're on our way, the better.'

He called for the landlord and started to make preparations to have Mr Epsom carried to his carriage. Soon Mr Epsom was stretched along one of the seats. 'Drink this,' said his friend, holding a flask of brandy to his mouth. 'You will feel better.'

Mr Epsom drank deeply and lay back. Then his face turned blue, and his heels slid from the seat and performed a mad tattoo on the floor. Quite soon after he died from the poisoned brandy he had drunk.

The carriage drove on and on until night fell. 'Stop here!' called the murderer, opening the trap in the roof.

He climbed out and looked up at a gibbet silhouetted against the moon. Three corpses in various stages of decomposition swung dismally on their chains. 'No one will notice an extra body, John,' he said to his coachman. 'I'll hand you up the body and you stand on the top of the coach and tie it up.'

His villainous coachman was too well trained and too well paid to ask such stupid questions as 'What body?'

Mr Epsom's corpse was undressed down to the breeches and shirt. They spattered and dirtied his shirt and tousled and muddied his hair until he looked like a common felon. Then, standing on top of the coach while his master steadied the horses, the coachman chained up the body alongside the other three.

'Now drive on,' said his master, 'and stop at the nearest inn and find out where the Earl of Greystone has his residence.'

'She's here!' trilled Effy. Amy jumped to her feet and she and her sister went down to the hall. A very tall girl was standing, blinking owlishly in the lamplight. Beside her stood a fat lady's maid.

Effy tripped forward, both hands held out in welcome. 'Greetings, Miss Vevian. I am Miss Effy Tribble and I hope you will be very happy with us.'

Clarissa looked down at the dainty white-haired Effy and felt large and awkward. All her newfound independence deserted her. 'Glad to meet you,' she mumbled. She seized Effy's hand and shook it. Effy let out a yelp of pain. 'There is no need to crush my hand, Miss Vevian,' she said.

'Sorry,' mumbled Clarissa, shuffling her feet.

A tall woman approached her. 'And I am Miss Amy,' she said. Clarissa looked relieved. Amy was almost as tall as she was herself. She was reassuringly harsh and plain. 'Good evening,' said Clarissa and dropped into a low curtsy. It was a very low curtsy indeed. Clarissa found she could not rise and sat down suddenly on the floor. The sisters helped her up. 'You are very tired from your journey, no doubt,' said Amy, feeling quite maternal. There was something about this tall girl that reminded Amy of herself. 'Give your bonnet and cloak to your maid. This,' said Amy, turning to introduce a gaunt, harsh-featured woman who was standing in the shadows of the hall, a little way away, 'is our maid, Baxter, who will show your maid to her quarters.'

Clarissa followed the sisters up the stairs and into the drawing room.

'Wine?' offered Effy.

Clarissa shuddered. 'No, I thank you.'

'Tea?'

'Oh yes, please.'

'Tell us,' asked Amy, 'what happened to your carriage and what has it to do with the Earl of Greystone?'

In a low clear voice, Clarissa recounted her adventures. When she got to the bit about bathing Tom's forehead with water from the sewer and then setting the carriage alight, Amy could control herself no longer. Her stifled snorts of laughter turned to outright guffaws. Clarissa reddened and Effy said quickly, 'Pay no heed to my sister. She is not herself.'

But Clarissa started to grin. Amy's laughter was infectious and soon the whole sorry tale began to strike her as being funnier and funnier. By the time she got to the bit about knocking Mr Epsom down the stairs, Amy was crying with laughter and Effy was rigid with shock.

'I see we'll deal famously,' said Amy at last, wiping her streaming eyes.

'Yes, quite,' said Effy repressively. 'When you have finished your tea, Miss Vevian, I will show you to your room. The hour is late. Have you dined?'

'Yes, thank you.'

When Clarissa had been seen to her room, Effy returned to the drawing room and looked severely at her sister. 'There is nothing to laugh at,' she said.

'Oh yes, there is,' hooted Amy. 'What a card!'

Effy sat down. 'Listen to me, Amy. I know now why she has been sent to us. She is gauche and clumsy and dangerously so. You must not encourage her by laughing at her. Her schooling must begin tomorrow. Smoking cheroots, indeed! I was never more shocked.'

'She's a great girl. Don't turn her into a simpering miss, Effy. You know what? I *like* her, and what's more, I bet this earl, Greystone, likes her too. He said he'd come here to settle accounts. Don't need to do that in person, you know. Could send a draft.'

'Do you think...' began Effy slowly.

'Bags of hope there,' said Amy cheerfully. 'Besides, we don't know that she usually goes on like she did on the journey. Parents should have been with her. Stands to reason, she'd be nervous and upset at having to go on such a long journey with only the maid for company.'

'Perhaps,' said Effy. 'But *red hair*. So unfortunate. And she is so very tall.'

'Better to make the most of her height,' said Amy shrewdly. 'She stoops a bit. Get the backboard on her and make her sit up straight. She could look regal.'

'But did you notice those freckles?' fretted Effy. 'Lemon and white of egg might do the trick.'

'I like freckles,' said Amy stubbornly.

Effy remembered Mr Haddon kissing Amy's hand. 'You like everything about Clarissa,' she said maliciously 'because she reminds you of yourself. But I do have to point out that you are still unwed, sister dear.'

'And all thanks to you,' said Amy furiously. 'Who forced me into turning down two whole proposals of marriage?'

'Not I. It was you who thought Squire Wraxall meant marriage when he was talking about another lady.'

'You're such a washed-out little thing,' said Amy waspishly. 'You don't understand women with bottom.'

'Bottom' in the Regency meant courage and gallantry. Effy deliberately misunderstood. 'You can't talk about women with bottoms,' she said. 'You're as flat as a board, front *and* back.'

'At least I don't have to wear a chin-strap every night. You've got a neck on you like a vulture.'

Effy began to cry.

'Oh, dear,' said Amy, instantly repentant.

'I say, don't cry. 'Member you said there was a necklace you wanted to buy? We could go tomorrow and get it if you like.'

Effy stopped crying and peeped over her handkerchief.

'Promise?'

'I promise,' said Amy cheerfully. Mr Haddon had kissed her hand and looked at her *so* – so Effy could say what she liked from now on!

The Earl of Greystone was feeling quite happy as he drove his half-sister and step-mother home after a visit to a neighbour. Amazingly, Clarissa's strategy had worked. He had announced that Peregrine would never go to school. To send the boy to Eton would be a waste of time and money, and furthermore, he was too spoilt to be fit company for other boys. Peregrine had tried to hold his breath and was slowly turning purple in the face when his heartless half-brother had walked from the room. By that evening, Angela had been weeping and begging the earl on her knees to let dear Peregrine go to Eton. The poor boy had set his heart on it, and on and on she went, until the earl had finally appeared reluctantly to give his ungracious permission. He privately resolved to raise heaven and earth to get the boy admitted as soon as possible, even if it had to be in the middle of term. Then he had broached the subject of the Grand Tour, quite casually, saying someone or other had suggested it for Tom, but of course Tom was such a stay-at-home it was probably out of the question. Tom defiantly and shrilly had demanded to be allowed to go.

The earl smiled and was wondering how Miss Vevian was faring in London. He looked forward to seeing her again and telling her how her plan had worked.

In a month's time, with any luck, he would be shot of both boys. It would mean a great deal of travel, first to Eton with Peregrine, and then to Oxford to hire a tutor to travel with Tom. Then he, would be free to take Bella to London.

Bella and Angela elected to retire for the night as soon as they got in the door. The earl decided to go to the saloon and sit quietly by the fire and read.

He had just settled himself comfortably with a book in his hand and a glass of wine at his elbow when the house was rent with shriek after shriek. Throwing down his book, he ran out of the room and up the stairs in the direction of the screams.

Bella and Angela were standing together in the passage outside Bella's room, clutching each other and staring in the open door. Bella opened her mouth to scream again. 'Stop that!' commanded the earl and pushed past them.

Bella's room was a wreck. Drawers hung at a drunken angle, with clothes hanging out of them. The mattress and the pillows on her bed had been sliced open. Her jewel box had been upended, bracelets and necklaces and brooches spilling out onto the floor. Even the upholstered chairs had been sliced open.

'My room is the same,' whimpered Angela.

The constable was called and the magistrate. The grounds and the outside of the house were examined, showing that the thief had climbed up the ivy into Bella's room and had then made his way to Angela's room through a connecting drawing room. Angela's room was only half-violated, as if the thief had been alarmed and had made his escape.

The servants were closely questioned but claimed to have neither seen nor heard anything. A footman did say he had been on his way to the bedchambers with baskets of logs when the butler stopped him and told him that the logs had already been taken up. The sound of his approach must have been what had alarmed the burglar.

The earl tried to calm Angela's hysterics, hitting on the solution at last by telling her she could choose new chairs and refurnish both rooms if she liked. Angela went off happily with Bella to draw plans for the redecoration.

In the busy weeks that followed, the earl kept in touch with the local magistrate to find out if any clue had been found as to the identity of the thief, but each time the magistrate reported that no one strange had been seen in the neighbourhood. What made it all so odd was that nothing of value had been taken and the magistrate suggested the reason might be spite. Perhaps the beautiful Lady Bella had unwittingly spurned some young gentleman at the Bath assemblies and this was his revenge.

The earl replied that Bella was always spurning someone or other but he doubted if any of the Bath Pump Room beaux would go to such lengths.

It took longer than he had expected to get Peregrine into Eton and to find a tutor for Tom and get that gentleman off on his travels. Angela fussed so and insisted that

Tom be kitted out with everything necessary for the journey, from a collapsible candlestick to lice-proof drawers.

At last the earl was able to send some of the servants ahead to open up the town house and planned to leave for London the following morning.

They had just finished an early dinner – or rather, the earl considered Angela's choice of four in the afternoon too early – and the earl had retired to the saloon when the butler announced that Sir Jason Pym was calling.

The earl looked up, startled. He and Sir Jason had been students at Oxford together and he had not clapped eyes on him since then. He remembered him as a shy young man with a stammer.

As Sir Jason walked in, Lord Greystone found it hard to recognize in this Exquisite the nervous undergraduate he had once known. Sir Jason was tall and slim and dressed very expensively. His cravat was perfection, his coat was of Bath superfine worn open over an ornately embroidered waistcoat. The heels of his boots were high and he wore gold spurs. His thin face was painted and his black eyes were sparkling and restless. He wore his hair long and powdered and tied at the nape of his neck with a black ribbon. It was not a style favoured by anyone under fifty, but the earl shrewdly judged that in this case the powdered hair was due to affectation rather than conservatism.

'What brings you calling so unexpectedly after all these years, Jason?' he said. 'Sit down by the fire and tell me about yourself.'

'I was in the neighbourhood,' drawled Sir Jason with no trace of his old stammer. 'Heard you lived here and thought, on impulse, you know, that I would call.'

'You are more than welcome,' said the earl. 'But we leave for London in the morning. I am taking my half-sister to town for the Season.'

At that moment, Angela and Bella entered. The earl introduced them. Both seemed delighted with Sir Jason, who said he was struck all of a heap with the beauty of the 'sisters', and Angela tittered and explained she was Bella's mother, at which Sir Jason cried, 'Never! It cannot be so.'

The earl reflected that Jason had turned out to be a tiresome fop.

'Have you any more divine beauties here?' cried Sir Jason.

'No, just us,' simpered Bella, hiding her face behind her fan.

'Strange.' A friend of mine claimed to have met a lady from your family, Crispin. He seemed vastly taken with her. He did not know her name, and when he asked the landlord at a certain posting-house, where this lady had spent the night, the landlord said that you, Crispin, had ordered the room for her and paid her bill.'

The earl frowned and then his face cleared. 'Oh, that would be the Honourable Clarissa Vevian. She stopped here on her road to London.' He flashed a warning look at Bella and Angela. He was sure they were dying to gossip about Clarissa who had set her own carriage on fire.

'Ah yes, a divine goddess, or so I am led to believe,' said Sir Jason.

'Nothing out of the common way,' said Angela waspishly. 'Great lummox of a girl with the reddest hair you have ever seen.'

'She is, let me see, Viscount Clarendon's daughter, is she not?' asked Sir Jason. 'I cannot remember where their house is in London.'

'Clarendon has a house in Bath,' said the earl. 'Miss Vevian is living with the ... in Holles Street.'

For some reason, he did not want to say she was living with the Tribbles. Angela and

75

Bella would then speculate out loud as to why Clarissa had been sent to the Tribbles. And everyone knew the Tribbles only sponsored girls who were a problem.

The conversation moved to other topics. By the time Sir Jason rose to leave, Angela and Bella were completely enchanted with him and the earl was devoutly hoping never to see him again. There was something slimy and oily about Sir Jason that he could not like.

To his dismay, he heard Sir Jason say he, too, would be at the Season and Angela replying that they would be delighted to have his company any time he cared to call.

The earl consoled himself with the thought that he would be glad if Bella married anyone at all and took herself out of his household and – pray God – took her mother with her.

3

Treason doth never prosper; what's the reason?
Why, if it prosper, none dare call it treason.
                          Sir John Harrington

While the Earl of Greystone was busy about his affairs in the country, Clarissa Vevian had not done very well in Town. The trouble lay in the person of Mr George Randolph.

Mr Randolph was a bachelor friend of Mr Haddon's, which put him in the same age bracket as the Tribbles and made him a source of excitement. He was small and slim and, unlike Mr Haddon, dressed in the very height of fashion. Like Mr Haddon, he was very rich, but he was also extravagant and liked to buy Amy and Effy expensive presents. Effy was charmed by him and Amy once more walked in flat shoes and with a slouch so as to suit his short height and wore those fussy, frilly girlish dresses which did not become her.

In the middle of all this, Clarissa felt like a neglected beanpole. She had already sent off one music teacher. He had tried to correct her playing by rapping her knuckles with a ruler. Clarissa had been too startled to think clearly and had snatched the ruler and brought it down with a crack on his head. The Italian tutor struggled on gamely, for he was poor and the wages were good. But ever since Clarissa had poured a cup of boiling-hot tea over his breeches, he had refused all refreshment and sat at the opposite end of the room from her to give her lessons. The dancing master, too, needed the money and so gave up dancing with her, but sat in a corner nursing his bandaged toes and calling out the figure of the dance while Clarissa leaped and pranced on her own. The curate, hired to give her religious instruction, was sorely alarmed that Clarissa refused point blank to believe in the existence of Hell. The curate was very fond of Hell and prided himself on his colourful descriptions.

The sisters were not totally unmindful of their duties. They examined her watercolours and her sewing in the evenings and took her out on calls during the day. Those calls were misery to Clarissa. She longed to find a friend among the other débutantes, but they huddled together and giggled and whispered, and most of them seemed to be barely over five feet in height.

Yvette, the French dressmaker, was her only comfort. Yvette, heavily pregnant, stitched away at a new wardrobe for Clarissa, encouraging the girl to draw sketches of what she would like. 'You cannot change other people, miss,' Yvette would say. 'You must change yourself inside first. It is you who makes you clumsy. *Ma foi!* It is difficult being so tall among all the little ladies, but hold your head high. Now me, I am the disgrace, *non?* I am to have the baby and no papa by my side. The servants here talk about me in shocked whispers. But I must ignore them, must I not?'

And so her soft voice would go on and Clarissa would leave her room feeling comforted and determined to do better and go out on another call where some dowager would hiss, 'Dear Miss Tribble, you've got your hands full with a great monster of a girl like that,' and she would begin to feel miserable all over again and drop something or fall over something.

Clarissa's maid, Hubbard, had sent all her jewellery off to be cleaned. She had seen the packet in the bottom of the box, had taken it out, scrubbed the box, and put it back again without looking inside. She assumed the packet contained love letters. All young ladies had love letters which they hid. It was none of Hubbard's business. When the jewellery was returned, she therefore arranged all the pieces back in the box with the packet once more underneath.

The Earl of Greystone was settled in his townhouse at last and free to call on Miss Clarissa Vevian. But no sooner was he on the point of setting out that a messenger arrived with a letter summoning him to the War Office. Wondering whether he was going to be asked to take up his old command, he went along.

He was given orders, but not the orders he had expected. He was told that it was believed the government papers which had recently been stolen had been taken by one of a band of aristocrats.

'I find that hard to believe,' said the earl. 'There was a lot of sympathy for Boney amongst the Whigs, but then when he made himself emperor, most got a disgust of him.'

'No,' said the tired old general facing him. 'No, my lord. I believe a number of them find treason a game. They enjoy the hazards and risks, and the money they are paid settles their gambling debts. We want you to go about in society and keep your ears and eyes open. Watch the ones with heavy debts closely. There are certain ones, you know, with estates mortgaged to the hilt who may suddenly settle their debts, having recently received a mysterious source of income. You may hear something, anything, which will lead us to them.'

They then settled back and fought old battles and talked about old friends.

That evening, Clarissa felt low and home-sick. She had gone out on a call with Miss Effy and the ladies had been talking of the Earl of Greystone and how he was in Town and what a vastly attractive man he was. Effy had said that the earl was a friend of Miss Vevian and Clarissa had been plied with eager questions. Not one lady present had looked on Clarissa as a rival.

She sat by the fire, her sewing lying un-heeded on her lap. The sisters, Mr Haddon, and Mr Randolph were playing bridge. They now played bridge most evenings. But for once, Mr Haddon's attention was not fully on the game. He kept glancing over at Clar-issa. Why, the girl was miserable! Did Amy know? But Miss Amy appeared totally taken up with Mr Randolph. She was wearing a very fine Norfolk shawl which Mr Randolph had given her. Mr Haddon reflected sourly that the Kashmir shawl *he* had given Amy was much finer. Amy had her grey-streaked hair dressed in pomaded girlish curls. It made her face look longer, and the jaunty, glossy curls looked like a wig.

He knew the attempted girlishness of Amy's appearance did not become her. Flat, heel-less shoes, for example, were all the rage, but before the advent of Mr Randolph, Amy had taken to wearing a low heel because she found it helped her posture. Now she shuffled about and stooped and did everything she could to diminish her height.

Effy was wearing a very pretty sapphire necklace. Mr Haddon hoped Mr Randolph had not bought it for her. It would be wicked if he had bought something so very expensive for Effy and not bought Amy a piece of jewellery as well. 'Your mind is wandering, Mr Haddon,' chided Amy.

'I am sorry,' he said in a low voice. 'I was worrying about Miss Vevian.'

'Nothing to worry about there,' whispered Amy. 'A trifle clumsy, but a thoroughly good girl.'

'She is unhappy.'

Amy put down her cards and stared at Mr Haddon. Effy made clucking noises of annoyance.

'But ... but ... are you *sure?*' asked Amy. 'I had not noticed.'

'No, you have eyes only for someone else,' said Mr Haddon coolly. 'And you are setting Miss Vevian a bad example.'

'Step outside,' said Amy sharply. 'My apologies, Mr Randolph.'

'Do not trouble to apologize to *me*,' said Effy, but the couple had risen and were already leaving the room.

'Kindly explain yourself,' said Amy when she and Mr Haddon were outside on the landing.

'I cannot help noticing that every evening Randolph and I call here to play bridge, Miss Vevian is always left out of things. You take her on calls, but you never take her to balls or parties. Why?'

Well, the answer to that one was that in all the glory of having *two* gentlemen for company, the Tribble sisters had all but forgotten about their responsibility to Clarissa, but Amy had no intention of telling him so.

'We have hired all the best tutors for her,' she said defensively.

'I am sure you have.'

'Then what did you mean when you said I was a bad example?'

'That was silly of me. Pray forget it.'

'I insist on knowing. You most certainly meant it.'

'Don't fly out at me then. The fact is that you are tall and Miss Vevian is tall. You, Miss Amy, had begun to adopt a dress and posture which suited your height and gave you a regal air. Since the arrival on the scene of my friend Randolph, you have started stooping again and wearing girlish clothes. He is the same age as you, you know.'

Amy's eyes filled with tears. 'What a cruel thing to say.'

'Prompted by affection for you and worry for Miss Vevian.'

Amy's heart melted. All she really heard was the 'affection for you' bit. 'I suppose we *have* neglected her,' she said slowly.

'What of Greystone? He is in Town. Has he called? Or, what is more to the point, have you sent cards and encouraged him to call?'

'No,' said Amy. 'You see, everyone's in a flutter about this earl and he is said to be devilishly handsome and Clarissa is not … well … precisely … well, she does not exactly have the type of looks to take the Town by storm.'

'She could have dignity and presence and a great deal of charm if perhaps someone would wish her to be exactly what she is and not keep trying to turn her into a simpering miss. Nothing,' said Mr Haddon severely, 'is worse than to see a large dignified woman stooping to ogle and simper.'

'Are you jealous of Mr Randolph, by any chance?'

'Of course I am,' said Mr Haddon. 'I am used to having your and Miss Effy's attention and do not like to take second place to my friend.'

He *would* have to mention Effy, thought Amy sourly.

'I'll try to do something about Miss Vevian tomorrow,' said Amy. 'Why! I'll even snap my fingers and conjure up the Earl of Greystone.'

There came a knocking on the street door.

Harris went to open it.

Amy and Mr Haddon leaned over the banisters.

The Earl of Greystone walked into the hall. His servant announced him and presented his master's card.

'Well, I'll be blowed,' said Amy. 'Back inside. Don't tell anyone. Let it be a surprise.'

'You're a sly dog,' said Mr Randolph to Mr Haddon. 'Whispering outside the door. What is going on?'

'Miss Amy has been performing magic,'

said Mr Haddon. 'She has conjured up a beau for Miss Vevian.'

Harris entered with a card on a tray. 'Show him up,' said Amy without looking at the card.

Effy rose in a flutter. 'Who is it? Is it really someone to see Miss Vevian? Don't be a tease, Amy. No one who is anyone calls at this hour.'

Harris flung open the door. 'The Earl of Greystone,' he announced.

Clarissa leaped to her feet and knocked her work-basket into the fire. With an exclamation of distress, she snatched at it and the burning work-basket rolled across the carpet. The earl seized a pair of tongs from the hearth, picked up the blazing work-basket and placed it on the fire.

'I am so very sorry,' said Clarissa wretchedly. 'I will buy you a new carpet. I insist.'

'Happens easily,' said Amy. 'Stupid things, work-baskets. Always rolling all over the place.' There were then introductions all round.

Amy looked curiously at the earl. He certainly was a magnificent creature. He was taller than Clarissa, with a lean figure, slim hips, and broad shoulders. Amy squinted down at his legs and heaved a sigh of pleasure. Perfect! He was wearing evening dress, midnight-blue coat with silver buttons, black silk knee breeches, white clocked stockings, and buckled shoes. He exuded an air of arrogance, wealth, and authority.

Not at all the sort of man, reflected Amy dismally, who would relish a clumsy wife. Poor Clarissa.

Wine was served and the company gathered around the fire.

'I am only just arrived in Town,' said the earl pleasantly, 'and meant to call this afternoon, but I had some urgent business to attend to. I really should have waited until tomorrow, but I was anxious to see Miss Vevian again.'

Watching Clarissa was like watching a drooping flower being put into water, thought Mr Haddon. At that last remark, Clarissa sat up straight and gave the earl a smile of singular sweetness. She seemed to come alive, her fine grey eyes sparkling and her tall slim figure, set off to advantage in a green velvet gown of somewhat old-fashioned cut, becoming almost pliant and willowy.

'I have some business to transact with Miss Vevian,' went on the earl. 'Would it be possible to have a few moments in private with her?'

'Of course,' said Amy hurriedly. 'We were playing bridge, you know.' The four resumed their places at the card table and the earl pulled his chair next to Clarissa's in front of the fire. He drew a paper from his pocket. 'If you will look at these figures, Miss Vevian,' he said, 'you will see I have put down a round sum to cover the cost of a new carriage and the clothes lost in the fire.'

'I should really not accept this, my lord,' said Clarissa. 'After all, it was I who set fire to the carriage, not your half-brother.'

'But you would not have done so had he not alarmed you with his silly tricks,' said the earl.

'I am very clumsy,' said Clarissa, 'as you have just witnessed.'

'Nonetheless, I am determined to pay.'

'Well, that is very good of you,' said Clarissa. 'If, perhaps, you could send the money for the carriage to my father, and give the money for my clothes to the Misses Tribble...?'

'Gladly. What is your father's direction?'

'Six hundred, Royal Crescent, Bath. We have a place in Wiltshire, but Papa is always in Bath.'

'I have news for you, Miss Vevian. I took

your good advice, with the result that Peregrine is now at Eton and Tom is on the Grand Tour. Now all you have to do is tell me how to find a husband for Bella and perhaps one for my stepmother as well.'

'They are both so very pretty,' said Clarissa. 'I am sure they do not need any help at all.'

'I think they do. You see, Bella is fickle. She enjoys breaking hearts, and Angela would disaffect any man with her humours and scenes. Bella does have a beau, but I fear he is not suitable. Well, perhaps he is but I confess there is something about the man I cannot like. Firstly, he is the same age as I, and Bella is only nineteen.'

'I ... I am nineteen,' said Clarissa, 'and...' She broke off in confusion. She had been about to say that anyone of his age was not too old, but then felt that a remark like that might appear a trifle fast. 'What is his name?' she asked.

'Sir Jason Pym. He was at Oxford with me, and a very shy, quiet young fellow he was, too. Now he is very *mondaine* and appears wealthy, whereas he was miserably poor at Oxford.'

'How came he by his knighthood?'

'Quite shockingly. Our Prince Regent has always had a penchant for older women and

... or so the gossip goes ... became enamoured of a respectable widow in Brighton some time ago. The widow would not take her quittance when the prince tired of her and threatened all sorts of scandals. She said she was expecting his child. She threatened to broadcast her plight in the newspapers. The prince was at his wit's end. She refused to accept money. She said he had deliberately seduced her and must recognize the baby when it was born as his own. Every pressure, was brought to bear on her, including threats, but she was immovable. Onto the scene came Jason. He got the prince's ear and said he could settle the matter. Grateful prince fell on his neck and promised him the earth if only this troublesome woman could be silenced.

'Lo and behold! Jason was successful. To everyone's surprise, the lady caved in and even accepted quite a modest sum for her silence. Jason was dubbed Sir Jason and found princely favour.'

'And what became of the widow?'

'Alas, her body was found on Brighton beach. It was assumed she had committed suicide.'

'Assumed?'

The earl sighed. 'Of course when anyone

gets close to the prince, there is always venomous gossip flying around, but a quite respectable source seemed to feel obliged to warn me this very afternoon that it had been whispered that before the prince even became involved with this widow that the widow had been seen in Jason's company, don't you see.'

'I don't quite...'

'Some nasty people began to hint that Jason had plotted with the woman to ensnare the prince and Jason had orchestrated her subsequent threats to expose the affair. It was even hinted he himself had promised to marry the widow if she did what he told her. Worst of all, it was rumoured that after receiving his knighthood, he killed the widow.'

'You must not let such a creature near your half-sister!'

'I have not seen Bella since I heard this worst piece of gossip, but I had already explained to her I did not approve of him. We have only just arrived in London, but he was our first caller. He paid me a visit in the country and I have a feeling he and Bella have been exchanging letters ever since.'

'Perhaps you should not have told her you did not approve of him,' said Clarissa thoughtfully. 'Did you tell her about the widow? I mean, not about him being suspected of murder, for you have only just learned that, but about his intimacy with her?'

'No, I simply said that Jason was a dangerous rake and to be avoided.'

'And so made him seem attractive,' said Clarissa.

'You have the right of it I had better tell her about the widow.'

'She will probably not believe you now, you know. She will think you are making it up. You really must encourage Bella to see as much of him as possible. If she is as fickle as you say, then she will soon tire of him. Forbidden fruit is always attractive.'

'How wise, Miss Vevian. Do you find forbidden fruit attractive?'

'I don't know,' said Clarissa candidly. 'No one has ever offered me any.'

'I hope they never do. All the same, I do not think I can allow Bella to spend any time at all in the company of a man who *may very* well be a murderer. Perhaps I should see Jason in private and tell him I forbid him to call. Now what have you been doing in London?'

'Schooling,' said Clarissa dismally. 'Nothing but schooling.'

'I thought you were past that age.'

'I am to be polished, like silver, in time for the Season. I am rubbed this way by the Italian tutor and that way by the dancing master and then buffed by various other gentlemen, but they can't seem to get a shine on me.'

'Perhaps because they do not recognize solid gold when they see it.'

'What a pretty thing to say! But then, I am sure you have had lots of practice.'

'Not I, I swear. The Pomfreys hold a ball next week. Do you attend?'

'I fear not. We do not go out in the evenings.'

'This is very naughty of the Tribbles. They are being paid to bring you out, not keep you in.'

'Perhaps they do not consider me ready yet.'

'Then I must persuade them. If the weather holds good, will you allow me to drive you tomorrow?'

'Yes,' said Clarissa, suddenly shy.

'I shall call for you at five.'

'I must have permission.'

'The Tribbles will be delighted to allow you to go. I am a great catch.'

Clarissa looked thoughtfully at the fire.

One little strand of pink silk hung over the charred remains of her work-basket. As she watched, it shrivelled up into black ash. 'That does sound a trifle vain, my lord.'

'Not in the slightest. I only speak the truth. It is nothing to do with my looks or talent, Miss Vevian, but everything to do with my title and fortune.'

'I do not have a title,' said Clarisa in a small voice, 'but I am an honourable and I do have a large fortune. I am not, however, beset with suitors.'

'What? Are all the Bath beaux so blind?'

'How flattering you are! Not blind. Merely anxious to stay alive a little bit longer. You see, it appears I am not only clumsy but dangerously so.'

'You are very young,' he said in a gentle voice. 'I used to be very nervous in society when I was your age. I shall never forget going to court for the first time. I fell over my sword.'

'Yes, but you did not stab anyone to death with it.'

'Come, Miss Vevian, I am sure you have not killed anyone.'

'Not yet,' said Clarissa gloomily.

'I must take my leave,' he said, getting to his feet. He bowed to the company, obtained permission from the delighted Tribbles to take Clarissa driving, and bowed his way out.

'Well,' began Effy and then squawked as Amy gave her a surreptitious kick. 'Don't refine too much on it,' muttered Amy, 'or you'll get her in a flutter and she might break something.'

Clarissa made her excuses and went up to her room. Her heart was beating hard. A handsome man was to take her out, not just any ordinary handsome man at that, but the Catch of the Season. Hubbard undressed her for bed, running around her, pulling tapes free, looking like a bad-tempered villager who did not want to dance round the maypole.

'I can do the rest, Hubbard,' said Clarissa, coming out of a dream. 'I wonder if Miss Yvette will have any of my clothes ready.'

'A disgrace, that's what it is,' grumbled Hubbard. 'A woman in her condition ought to have been turned out in the streets where she belongs. But that's the French for you.'

'And that's a lack of Christian compassion for you,' snapped Clarissa, who had grown quite fond of the French dressmaker. 'Be off with you, Hubbard, and say your prayers.'

Clarissa was so excited, she thought she

would not be able to sleep, but she soon plunged down into the depths of a pleasant dream where she was dancing at Almack's and everyone was exclaiming at the intricacy and style of her steps.

In her dream, the quadrille finished and she saw the Earl of Greystone approaching her. He had a smile in his eyes. He held out his hand. She went to take it, but a little fluffy miss with bobbing curls and big blue eyes moved in front of her. The earl's arm encircled the fluffy miss's waist and they moved off together.

Somewhere in the depths of her dream, Clarissa told herself it was only a dream and that she ought to wake up. She opened her eyes and looked bleakly up at the ceiling. She remembered that fluffy creature. Her name had been Chloris Deveney. Clarissa had been sent to a seminary in Bath for a year but had only lasted a few months. She had insisted on having a bath and had gone to sleep in it. She had had a nightmare and had rolled out of the tin bath, upsetting the contents onto the floor, and water had seeped down and ruined the ceiling of the assembly room underneath. Chloris had been at the seminary at the same time. She was everything Clarissa was not, small and dainty and deft.

Clarissa was brought abruptly back to the present by the feeling that there was someone in her room. At first she only sensed a presence. Then she wrinkled her nose. There was a faint smell of patchouli. Then she heard the creak of a floorboard and quick shallow breathing.

'Who's there?' she cried, starting up.

There was a little gasp and then the soft opening and closing of the door.

'Help!' shouted Clarissa at the top of her voice. She climbed from the bed and lit a branch of candles with a spill which she thrust between the bars of the still-glowing fire.

She looked wildly about. Everything was in its place. Nothing had been disturbed.

The door opened and Amy erupted into the room, clad in a voluminous nightgown. Effy appeared behind her, her head covered in curl-papers.

'There was someone in my room,' said Clarissa.

'You must have been dreaming,' said Amy crossly. 'Who would want to come into your room?'

'I don't know. But there was definitely someone here,' said Clarissa stubbornly.

'Is anything the matter?' came Harris the

butler's voice from the passage outside.

Amy turned round. 'Miss Vevian claims there was someone in her room.'

'No one could have got into the house,' said Harris. 'With so many burglaries, I go round each night before retiring and check that everything is locked and bolted.'

'Then it must have been one of the servants,' exclaimed Clarissa.

'I cannot believe that,' said Harris firmly. 'We have a new housekeeper, Mrs Loomis, who came with excellent references. Apart from that, there are no new servants, and each one is highly respectable. After that business with Frank, I made it my job to check out all references personally,'

Frank, an over-ambitious footman, had left them after trying to stir up rebellion in the servants' hall.

'You are tired, Miss Vevian,' said Amy firmly. 'Go back to sleep. I shall go round with Harris and make sure that everything is secure.'

Left on her own again, Clarissa paced up and down. Then she went and locked her door before climbing into bed. It had not been a dream, of that she was sure.

But when she awoke next morning to see the sun streaming in the window, the events of the night before seemed unreal. The day was fine and a handsome man was to take her driving. She hoped Yvette had at least one gown ready!

4

The sky is glowing in one ruddy sheet;
A cry of fire! resounds from door to door;
And westward still the thronging people pour;
The turncock hastens to F. P. six feet,
And quick unlocks the fountains of the street;
With rumbling engines, with increasing roar,
Thunder along to luckless Number Four.

Thomas Hood

Bella and her mother were companionably drinking tea and eating toast. Angela often boasted they were more like sisters than mother and daughter. 'And have you heard from Sir Jason?' asked Angela.

'He is to call today,' Bella pouted. 'He sent such delicious letters that my poor heart was quite aflutter, but I confess when I actually clapped eyes on him again, he seemed a sorry creature. What do we do this evening?'

'Nothing,' said Angela with a shrug. 'We have many invitations for the next few weeks but nothing for the immediate present. Where is Crispin?'

'He's gone out, or so the servants tell me.' The butler entered and handed Bella a letter. 'This came by hand, my lady,' he said.

'Bound to be something boring,' said Bella, crackling open the seal. 'Dear me, it is from Sir Jason. What does he say?' Her eyes rapidly scanned the page and then she threw the letter down. 'Well, Mama, if this isn't the outside of enough!'

'What is wrong?'

'My half-brother, Crispin, has taken it on himself to call on poor Sir Jason this morning and to tell him to stay away from me in future! How dare he! You must speak to him, Mama.'

'Well, to be sure, it is all very *dégoûtant, ma chérie*. But you was just saying as how you were tired of the creature.'

'I shall make up my own mind as to whom I shall see or not see.'

Angela sighed. 'It's of no use arguing with Crispin.'

'No,' said Bella slowly. 'But I shall do as I please.'

'Oh, do not do anything to antagonize Crispin. He does hold the purse-strings, you know.'

'Pooh! His disapproval has quite re-animated my affections towards Sir Jason.'

'I hear that Vevian creature is in town. She is one of the Tribbles' bad ladies.'

'Who are the Tribbles and what have they to do with bad ladies?'

'They advertise in a most vulgar way. They sponsor young females of good *ton* at the Season, females who have hitherto proved difficult to puff off.'

'And what is Miss Vevian's deep dark secret?'

'I had it from that Mrs Deveney we met in Portugal Street yesterday evening when we went out to take the air. Was you not attending?'

'No, she seemed a tiresome gossip.'

'Well, her daughter, Chloris, attended a seminary in Bath and this Clarissa Vevian was there at the same time. Mrs Deveney says she is so clumsy, she is a walking threat to any who come nigh.'

Bella let out a delighted trill of laughter. 'How wonderful. Nothing to fear there. You know what a martinet Crispin is.'

To Clarissa's delight, Yvette had finished a carriage dress of dull green velvet trimmed with gold braid. It had epaulettes, all in the latest fashion, and a saucy shako had been bought to go with it. Under Yvette's supervision, Hubbard pomaded Clarissa's hair and curled it in such a way that the shako could be worn at a rakish angle and reveal a luxuriant fall of curls on the right-hand side of her head.

Amy came in to watch the preparations and expressed her approval. 'What a difference clothes make,' she said, 'and Lord Greystone's generous sum of money will be able to furnish you with many more.'

'I could make a similar dress for you, Miss Amy,' said Yvette. 'This style *à la militaire* is very suitable for tall ladies. If one is tall, one must be very *grande dame*.'

'I have many fine clothes, Yvette,' said Amy, delicately averting her eyes from the dressmaker's swollen girth. 'You must rest a great deal now.'

'When is...?' began Clarissa and then blushed as Hubbard and Amy frowned at her. She had been about to ask when Yvette's baby was due to arrive but mentioning birth or babies was just as indelicate as mentioning breeches or legs. She did not know that broad-spoken Amy would normally have cheerfully discussed every facet of Yvette's condition, but Mr Haddon had given her a guilty conscience and she was once more determined to take her job of mentor and chaperone seriously.

'We have not been concentrating on your deportment, Miss Vevian,' said Amy. 'You must hold yourself very straight or we will need to put the backboard on you.'

'Yes, it is important to stand straight,' said Yvette with a sly look at Amy, who had taken to slouching of late in an attempt to bring herself down to Mr Randolph's size.

'Now, I assume you know the etiquette of driving in a carriage,' went on Amy, ignoring Yvette. 'When introduced to people in the Park, you shake hands with your equals if the carriages are close enough, and confine yourself to a common nod if the people are your social inferiors. Do not wait for the gentleman to hand you up. He needs to control the horses. Mount gracefully. Do not discuss politics whatever you do. Some of the most unexpected people are Whigs,' said Amy, who was a Tory. 'Do not discuss Napoleon or anything of a military nature. Avoid talking about either religion or the poor. Religion is an inflammatory subject and the poor, a depressing one. You may talk about gowns and fashions and the weather. Above all, do not say anything intelligent. Gentlemen abhor intelligent women. Aim for frailty and weakness of body and mind.

It is expected of us.'

'Lord Greystone was good enough to say he appreciated my advice on certain family matters,' said Clarissa.

'Oh, that is quite suitable. Talk of aunts and cousins and things like that. You can also talk of pets, if you have any. A love of a pug dog shows the correct amount of sensibility, though,' said Amy with a burst of candour, 'I cannot abide the wheezing, vomiting, urinating creatures myself.'

'I shall remember what you say,' said Clarissa with an anxious look at the clock. 'It lacks only a few minutes to five. Should I not go down and wait in the hall?'

'No. He will not want to leave his cattle standing for very long outside, but a certain maidenly hesitation is called for. You wait here and we will call you.'

When they had left, Clarissa sat in an agony of anticipation. What if he did not come?

Then a footman scratched at the door and called, 'The Earl of Greystone is arrived, miss.'

Clarissa shot from the room with such energy that she nearly flattened the footman. She ran to the stairs and headlong down them, nearly lost her footing on the last few stairs and clutched desperately on to the banisters.

Effy rolled her eyes to heaven. The earl turned away and began to talk to Amy, giving Clarissa a chance to compose herself.

Clarissa was very subdued as she sat beside him in his carriage. Why couldn't she have made a stately entrance?

At a crossing, a light gig darted in front of them and the earl's horses reared and plunged. He controlled them and spoke to them calmly and firmly. He had immediately placed an arm across Clarissa so she would not fall out. That arm pressed under her bust made Clarissa feel shaky.

'Are you all right?' he asked when they moved off again.

'Yes, my lord,' said Clarissa.

'Utter fool. Shouldn't be allowed on the road. I would make them all pass exams before they were allowed out on the King's Highway. Are you sure you are all right? You look a trifle pale.'

'Yes, yes. You see, I did not have enough sleep last night.'

'Why was that?'

'Only a silly dream. I was sure I woke up and that there was someone in my room. I cried for help and roused the household and was made to feel very silly.'

'All this rich London food. Tell me about it.'

'What? Dinner?'

'No, silly, your dream.'

'It was so very real. I dreamt I was dancing and ... and ... oh, you know the way embarrassing things can happen in dreams.'

'Quite. I once had a dream that I was in the royal drawing room minus ... er ... a certain part of my clothing.'

'Oh,' said Clarissa. She blushed furiously at the wicked picture he had conjured up, remembered what he had looked like naked, and said weakly, 'Oh' again.

'Anyway, go on about your dream.'

'When this embarrassing thing happened in my dream,' said Clarissa, 'I suddenly knew I was dreaming and should wake up. I opened my eyes and then I felt a presence in my bed-chamber. I called out, "Who's there?" and there was a little gasp and then I heard the door open and close.'

'And then what happened?'

'I climbed from the bed and lit a branch of candles and held it up. Nothing had been disturbed. Then I shouted for help.'

'I do not think you were dreaming at all,' he said. 'Probably one of the servants was trying to rob you.'

'I did think that, but Harris, the butler, you know, assured me all the servants' references had been checked.'

'I would be on my guard, nonetheless.'

'What a very comforting gentleman you are,' said Clarissa with a burst of candour. 'I am so used to being thought silly, you see.'

'I don't think I could ever damn you as silly, Miss Vevian.'

Clarissa let out a sigh of pure pleasure. When they stopped several times beside carriages in the Park and he introduced her to various members of society, she behaved beautifully. She felt like quite a different person and, beside him, almost small.

But her happiness was not to last much longer. A smart barouche approached them, bearing not only Lady Bella and Angela, Dowager Countess of Greystone, but Mrs Deveney and her daughter Chloris.

Lady Bella was bad enough, thought Clarissa dismally, but at least she was the earl's half-sister. Chloris was another matter entirely. She was as dainty and fragile as Clarissa remembered her to be. Her fair fluffy curls were topped by a ridiculously small straw hat. Her huge blue eyes looked up caressingly at the earl. They all talked for a little and then the earl drove on. 'Pretty little thing, that Miss Deveney.'

'Yes, very,' said Clarissa in a colourless voice. 'I knew her in Bath. We attended the same seminary. Of course I did not know her very long, for I was asked to leave.'

'And why was that?'

'A wretched accident. I upset the bathwater. You see, I fell asleep in the bath. The water soaked through the floor and ruined the ceiling below. The floor could not have been very sound, for the water disappeared through it so quickly. I tore down my bedroom curtains to mop up the mess, but there was little I could do.

'I do not think you are clumsy,' he said gently. 'Perhaps very unlucky. It is an accident that could have easily happened to one of the other young misses.'

'Not exactly. It was considered most odd in me to want a bath in the first place. Baths are really only for medicinal purposes, you know.'

'Not in my case, Miss Vevian. I have a French bath with a machine at the head of it which heats the water so that my servants do not have to carry boiling water up from the kitchens. In fact, I am considering improvements to my town house at the end of the Season so that water will be pumped up to all the rooms.'

'But only three times a week in London, or so I have discovered,' said Clarissa.

'Perhaps things will change soon. There are so many new inventions. Now if everyone in London Town were as clean as you, Miss Vevian, we should be in a sorry mess. Fifty thousand hogsheads of water are pumped up by that antiquated machinery on London Bridge every twenty-four hours, although it is only distributed to the houses three times a week on a rota system. That does not go very far as it is. Imagine if the whole population took to keeping themselves clean for a change.'

'Then they would be forced to do something,' said Clarissa. 'Necessity breeds invention.'

'You should have been a politician.'

'Not I. I lack the necessary zeal.'

'As do most of the members of the Houses of Parliament. By the way, what do you think of Napoleon now?'

'Horrid, detestable man,' said Clarissa.

'And yet even Wellington allows he is a great military leader. He even has his followers in this country.'

'I suppose spy fever will start up again,'

said Clarissa. 'I can remember, when I was small, seeing a perfectly respectable man being arrested because he had been studying ships in the Avon through a telescope. He was accused of spying – that was, until they discovered he was a magistrate. Why would anyone want to betray their country?'

'For money.'

'But poor people are not in a position to ferret out military secrets.'

'There are members of the *ton* beset by gambling debts. They have ruined their estates and beggared their tenants, but they would do anything rather than be reduced to the straits to which they themselves have reduced so many. But these are serious matters for a sunny day. Are you going to that ball?'

'I didn't ask about it,' said Clarissa, reflecting that she had not been able to think of anything else that day other than going out driving with him.

'I shall come in for a few moments when we go back. I think you should start your debut right away. If the Tribbles and those two gentlemen wish to play cards of an evening, they can play in my home for a change. I shall invite you all to dinner tomorrow night.'

'That would be wonderful,' said Clarissa,

clasping her hands. 'Why are you so kind to me?'

'Because I am sorry for you.'

The radiance vanished from her face and he cursed inwardly. But if he said he wanted to see her again very soon then she might decide his intentions were serious and that would be awkward.

They drove back in silence. Clarissa thought miserably that he might have forgotten about his invitation, but he entered the house with her and requested to see the Tribbles in private.

Amy was already feeling guilty about Clarissa. Now she was made to feel even more guilty. The earl politely asked why it was Miss Vevian had not appeared at any balls or parties if they were supposed to be bringing her out.

'Because she is not ready yet,' said Effy.

'Nonsense. She has delightful manners. Pray, bring her to dinner at my home tomorrow evening. Mr Haddon and Mr Randolph are invited as well – that is, if they are free to accept at such short notice.'

'We are delighted to accept your invitation,' said Amy. 'I do hope we are not putting the dear dowager countess to any trouble.'

'Not in the slightest. Angela will be delighted.'

'I was never more furious in my life, Bella,' said Angela, as she perched on the end of her daughter's bed that evening. 'Things look bad. Very bad.'

'Great clumsy maypole. What can he see in her?'

'I don't think he sees anything in her,' said Angela slowly. 'I think he is sorry for her. He's always helping lame ducks. Do you remember that tenant farmer, whatever the man's name was? His son had the smallpox and Crispin must needs put his life, and ours, at risk by accompanying the physician and sitting with the boy. I pointed out that if the boy died, there would be no one to inherit the farm, the farm would revert to the estate, and he could sell it at a fine profit. He called me vulgar. Me! Perhaps he finds her social gaffes endearing. Oh, that we could make her commit some awful accident. That would surely give him a disgust of her.'

'What?' said Bella, hugging her knees and looking at her mother with admiration.

'Crispin has gone to bed. Come down to the drawing room and let us see if we can think of something.'

Bella pulled on a wrapper and followed her mother downstairs. Angela paced about the drawing room, looking at this and that. 'I wanted Crispin to redecorate this room. The furniture is so old and unfashionable,' said Angela, looking at a set of Chippendale chairs with loathing. 'And look at the curtains. Dingy, my dear. Positively dingy. I've prayed that this room would go on fire...'

She stopped in her tracks. 'That's it. We'll get clumsy Clarissa to set the room on fire.'

'Now how can we do that, Mama,' said Bella crossly. 'We can hardly hand her a torch and tell her to apply it to the curtains.'

'Wait a bit! Say we soaked the ends of these curtains in oil and say we contrived to light the end of her scarf...'

'She may not be wearing a scarf.'

'Nonsense, every fashionable woman wears one of those long scarf things. Say we contrive to set it alight and place her chair right against the curtains... Yes. I think that might do the trick.'

'That's all very well, but what of our things? What if the whole house goes up in flames?'

'Then we each get a new wardrobe, silly.'

'But what of our jewellery and fine lace?'

'Oh, dear. Let me think.' Angela sat down and stared into space. 'We'll just need to tell our maids that I have a premonition and they are to remove the boxes to the hall during dinner for safety.'

'Is the house insured?'

'Of course. Did you not notice the plaque outside the front door? It is insured with the Phoenix.'

No one could complain of want of insurance companies in Regency London. There existed sixteen fire-insurance companies – The Sun, Phoenix, Royal Exchange, Hand in Hand, Westminister, London, Union, British, Imperial, Globe, County, Hope, Atlas, Pelican, Albion and Eagle. Each fire-insurance company had its badge, which was stamped out in sheet lead, painted and gilt, and then nailed onto the house insured.

'And I happen to know he is paying a Doubly Hazardous Insurance of five shillings per cent,' said Angela, 'so there will be plenty of money to buy what we want!'

The guilt-stricken Tribble sisters descended on Clarissa the following day, each one anxious to correct her faults in as short a time as possible. So Clarissa, who had hoped to have some time at leisure to dream about the evening ahead, was strapped into a backboard, a pile of books was placed on her head, and she was told to pour tea without spilling a drop. 'I hear there is a man on Tower Hill who chains himself up, puts himself in a sack, and then contrives to escape from it,' said Clarissa. 'A little more of your training, ladies, and I shall be set to rival him.'

Amy ignored her. 'Yes, now, pour the tea. No! Don't rush at things. Look how you hurtled down the stairs yesterday. Slow movements. Slow and elegant. Here!' She turned on a metronome. 'Now, I have set this to a slow beat. Orchestrate all your movements to its beat. Always raise the cup and saucer in your one hand, never leave it lying on the table, and pour. Try to achieve a swan-neck bend to your arm. Pass round the cakes. Curve your arm. Don't have your elbows sticking out. Oh! Whoresons of strumpets!'

Clarissa had upended the plate of cakes in Amy's lap.

'Amy!' admonished Effy. 'Such language.'

'May I take this backboard off?' pleaded Clarissa. 'It is so heavy. I promise to sit up straight.'

'Oh, very well,' said Effy, unstrapping the cumbersome board. 'But remember, your back should never touch the back of your chair. Don't lounge. Only gentlemen are allowed to lounge.'

'What is she going to do after dinner?' asked Amy. 'It would be a good idea to keep her hands occupied.'

'True,' said Effy. 'Now a little netting-box is very pretty and ladylike. She could be netting a purse.'

'The very thing,' said Amy. 'But perhaps we are wasting time. *She* won't be presiding over the tea-tray. The countess will do that. How she behaves at the dinner table is more important.'

Effy rang the bell and ordered dinner to be served, although it was only eleven in the morning. Harris complained that nothing was ready but Effy told him to bring cold meats and salad. 'You take your fork, Miss Vevian,' said Effy, 'and you cut up a little of each item on your plate and make sure you have a selection of each on your fork at once. That is the fashion.'

'I am not hungry,' said Clarissa miserably.

'Force yourself,' said Amy heartlessly. 'Now, pretend I am a gentleman at the table. I raise my glass. I say, "Will you take wine with me, Miss Vevian?" You raise your glass to him and smile so ... and drink. No, not all at once! Refill her glass, Harris. Now, you raise your glass to the gentleman to indicate you wish him to take wine with you. And so it goes on throughout the meal.'

And so it went on throughout the day. By evening, Clarissa felt slightly sick, very tired, and totally bewildered.

She was dressed in a white silk gown with a gold silk overdress, fastened at the front with gold-and-pearl clasps. Pearls were wound through her thick red tresses and a little rouge had been applied to her lips. The high-waisted style became her very well. A long scarf of gold tissue was draped about her shoulders, the ends falling to the floor.

Amy and Effy were delighted with her appearance. 'It is a pity about the freckles,' said Effy 'but a light dusting of pearl powder stops them from showing up so much.'

And then Mr Haddon and Mr Randolph arrived to escort the ladies. Clarissa over-heard Mr Randolph say, 'Miss Vevian looks really regal. Those pearls wound through her tresses make her look like a queen. You should be proud of your handiwork, ladies.'

A little glow started somewhere in the pit of Clarissa's stomach. For the first time, she saw that the Tribbles were really proud of her appearance. All the upsets of the day melted away and she walked from the house feeling attractive and admired.

Even the sight of Chloris Deveney, who had also been invited, did little to dampen Clarissa's newfound confidence. She was seated next to the earl at the dinner table and managed to cope with the meal perfectly, apart from knocking some peas onto the floor, grinding them into the carpet with her foot in the hope that the earl would not notice, and then finding out that he had.

Angela rose at the end of the meal to lead the ladies to the drawing room. Clarissa was accompanied by Amy, who seemed determined to stick close to her. Amy had decided that pretty, dainty Bella, her pretty, dainty mother, and pretty, dainty Chloris might cause Clarissa to start shuffling and stooping again, and so she kept beside her in the hope that her own tall figure would give Clarissa confidence. Amy was pleased with her own appearance. Once more she wore little heels on her shoes and her gown was of deep purple velvet. It was wonderful to feel warm after shivering in those frippery muslins.

'Sit here, dear Miss Vevian,' said Angela, indicating a chair in front of the drawn window curtains.

Clarissa sat down. Amy made to sit beside

her. 'No, no,' said Angela, 'you must allow me the pleasure of conversing with Miss Vevian.'

Clarissa sniffed the air. 'There is a strong smell of oil, my lady,' she said. 'Are you sure one of the lamps is not leaking?'

'I scented this room with rose-water myself,' said Angela stiffly.

Clarissa, flustered, apologized.

She looked across the room and caught Chloris staring at her with a rather nasty look in her eyes. Now what have I done? thought Clarissa miserably.

She would have been amazed if she had known that Chloris was bitterly jealous of her. In vain did Chloris try to remind herself that red hair was not fashionable. The rich coils and curls of Clarissa's tresses, set off by the soft gleam of the strings of pearls wound through them, were enough to set any man dreaming. Her gown had been cut to show off the splendour of her white bosom. Her elbows were perfect. Chloris, whose elbows were like nutmeg graters, wondered what Clarissa used to keep them so smooth and white. Everyone knew that any man could be seduced by the sight of a perfect pair of elbows. But Clarissa did have big feet, reflected Chloris, looking down at her own small plump feet in satisfaction. Of course, there was no denying Clarissa's feet were very well shaped and set off to advantage in a pair of gilt Roman sandals.

'Shall we promenade about the room, Miss Vevian?' asked the countess.

'Gladly.' Clarissa put down the netting-box she had just drawn out of her reticule and proceeded to walk up and down with Angela. She caught Amy's eye and walked slowly and kept her head up. Angela raised her hand as she passed Bella. It was a signal to remind her daughter that as soon as the gentlemen entered the room, she was to contrive to set Clarissa's long gauze scarf alight, but to make it look as if Clarissa had carelessly allowed it to float out over a candle. It was to be done as they were promenading back towards the chair by the curtains. With any luck, Clarissa would throw her scarf in the direction of the curtains.

The room was very hot, thought Clarissa. The fire was roaring up the chimney and there seemed to be lighted candles everywhere. Not only were there candles blazing in the candelabrum over her head, but there were candles burning on sticks on various low tables. Quite dangerous, thought Clarissa, making sure neither her dress nor her scarf went anywhere near one of the many burning flames.

Angela's plan was totally hare-brained. Although she had soaked the bottoms of the curtains in oil and the floorboards around the edges of the room, there was no reason why Clarissa should simply not stamp out the flames of her scarf – providing, of course, Bella managed to light it unseen.

But Bella was helped by the effect the arrival of the gentlemen had on the ladies. Clarissa had eyes only for the earl, as had Chloris Deveney and her mother. Amy and Effy each suspected Angela of having designs on either Mr Haddon or Mr Randolph and both rushed forward to stake their claim to one or the other gentleman.

Bella deftly caught one end of Clarissa's scarf and held it over a candle. It took but a second.

'You have set yourself alight!' screamed Bella, seizing Clarissa and pretending to try to beat out the flames as she edged Clarissa towards the window. Clarissa tore off the scarf. The now blazing scarf landed on the floorboards by the window. The next moment, there was a roaring wall of flame.

The earl caught Clarissa around the waist and dragged her back. 'Everyone out,' he called. 'Out of the room.'

When they were all out, he slammed the door shut and took off his coat and stuffed it along the bottom: 'If we can starve the room of oxygen, the fire might extinguish itself,' he said.

Servants had gone off running to fetch the fire brigade.

The earl drove them all before him out into the street. 'Did you leave any windows in the drawing room open?' he snapped at Angela.

'No,' said Angela. 'The shutters are closed tight as well.'

'Good!'

'I didn't know that,' whispered Angela fiercely to Bella when the earl had moved away. 'I thought air would put the fire out.'

The men of the Phoenix Fire Brigade came charging up the street, pulling their manual fire-engine. The fire-plug in the street was pulled up. The Phoenix boasted the most powerful fire-engine of the time, but it could only throw a ton of water a minute through a three-quarter-inch nozzle. But other pumps were already being wheeled up in front of the house. 'Get at it, men,' screamed the fire chief. 'This is a five-shilling-per-cent job!'

'Take the hose inside,' shouted the earl. 'The shutters are closed.' The firemen ran inside and up the stairs. The servants formed a long line up the stairs, passing buckets of water from hand to hand. The earl opened the drawing-room door and fell back as a great cloud of black smoke rolled out.

Down in the street, everyone waited anxiously. A large crowd was gathering. A gingerbread man was already hawking his wares and a juggler was entertaining the gathering.

Clarissa felt sick with shame. She had done it again. Amy put a comforting arm about her. She was clumsy herself and knew how easy it was to cause disaster with one thoughtless movement.

'I think,' said Mr Haddon, coming up to Amy, 'that perhaps it might be a good idea to offer to house the earl and his party.'

'Yes,' said Amy dismally. It was the only thing to be done, she realized that. But to have Angela with her delicate flirty ways in residence? No more pleasant card evenings. It was too bad. But she gritted her teeth, and when the earl appeared again, she reluctantly invited him to stay.

'Thank you,' said the earl. 'The fire is out,

by some miracle. Only the drawing room is damaged. Mr Haddon, Mr Randolph, if you will escort the ladies to Holles Street, my servants will follow with the luggage.' He broke off. Bella's lady's maid and Angela's lady's maid were standing together with jewel boxes and lace boxes at their feet.

'You are fortunate your maids got those out,' he said.

'Oh, yes,' said Angela. 'So brave of them to go and fetch them.'

'It was my lady's premonition,' said Angela's lady's maid. 'She had a dream there might be a fire and told us to have the jewel boxes and lace boxes standing ready in the hall.'

'Silly goose,' said Angela. 'I said no such thing.'

'We will talk about the fire later,' said the earl curtly. 'Off with you.' He turned to a servant. 'Make sure those firemen keep all the other doors in the house tight shut until the smoke dies down or all our clothes will be ruined.'

Soon the party was assembled in the Tribbles' drawing room. 'So brave of you to take on such *dangerous* charges,' murmured Angela to Effy. 'I mean, such a clumsy and stupid thing to do!'

Clarissa heard her and sat miserably with her head hanging. Amy was wondering how much all this would cost. The building was insured, but now she would have to provide food and wine for the earl, his stepmother, and half-sister.

Mr Haddon and Mr Randolph had returned to the earl's home to see what they could do. Mrs Deveney and Chloris, who had accompanied the stricken party to Holles Street, finally took their leave.

At midnight, the earl came into the drawing room with Mr Haddon and Mr Randolph. 'It might have been worse,' he said.

'I am so very sorry,' whispered Clarissa brokenly. 'I am a danger to society.' She turned to Amy and Effy. 'I think, you know, I should go home to Bath.'

'What a very good idea,' said Angela brightly.

The earl looked at her for a long time and then his gaze turned to Bella. Then he said, 'Please retire and take Bella with you. There are some things I wish to discuss in private with the Misses Tribble. Gentlemen' – to Mr Haddon and Mr Randolph – 'I would be grateful if you too could leave me in private with these ladies.'

Clarissa began to tremble. Amy walked

over to where Clarissa was sitting on the sofa and sat down and put an arm about her.

The earl closed the drawing-room door and faced the small group.

'Tell me exactly what happened, Miss Vevian, and leave nothing out.'

'I ... I...' began Clarissa and burst into tears.

'Give her some brandy,' said the earl. He waited patiently while Amy soothed Clarissa, patted her clumsily on the back, and then held a glass of brandy to her lips.

'Now, Miss Vevian,' said the earl.

'I went to the drawing room after dinner with the ladies,' said Clarissa in a tired, flat voice. 'Lady Angela asked me to sit by the window. I took out my netting-box and then she asked me if I would promenade with her. I was nervous because I had asked her if one of her lamps might be leaking – the room smelt of oil, you see – and Lady Angela said she had scented the room that day with rose-water. I felt very gauche and that may have been what made me clumsy. There were so many candles burning on low tables that I did try to be careful. Then ... let me see ... you, my lord, and the other gentlemen came into the room and Lady Bella cried out I was on fire and hustled me across the room...'

'In the direction of the window?' asked the earl.

'Why, yes. But I am not quite clear in my mind. Suddenly there was this roaring sheet of flame and you know the rest.'

'Yes, I do know the rest,' said the earl, obviously furious.

Amy got to her feet and stood between the earl and Clarissa. 'Careful, my lord,' she said quietly. 'Miss Vevian is at the end of her tether as it is.'

'And I am at the end of mine,' he raged. 'Do you not see what happened? No, of course not. How can you? Angela had been plaguing me to buy new furnishings for the drawing room, which she regards as her pre-serve. I refused. I think she soaked the floor-boards and curtains in oil and then staged that so-called accident. It shames me to tell you this, ladies. Miss Vevian, I beg you to forgive me, or rather to forgive my wretched family.' He moved round Amy and knelt in front of Clarissa and looked into her tearful face.

'You mean I am not responsible?' asked Clarissa.

'No, Miss Vevian. You are the victim of a malicious plot.'

129

Clarissa started to smile, a wide happy smile.

He got to his feet. 'Excuse me, ladies,' he said. 'I must see my relatives immediately.'

He went out and closed the door. There was a long silence.

Then, 'Hurray!' cried Amy, slumping down in a chair and kicking off her shoes. 'Champagne! Get Harris and bring champagne. My dear Clarissa, I may call you that, may I not? My dear, dear Clarissa, the bad days are over for you. We shall drink to your success at the Season. Think, my chuck, in all your misspent life, you must admit you have never done anything half as bad as the Dowager Countess of Greystone.'

Harris brought in champagne. The three ladies raised their glasses. 'To the best Season the Tribbles ever had!' cried Amy.

They solemnly drank the toast while from above came the sound of noisy weeping and the Earl of Greystone's voice raised in anger.

5

O never let the lying poets be believed,
who 'tice men from the cheerful haunts
of streets... A garden was the
primitive prison till man with
promethean felicity and boldness
luckily sinned himself out of it. Thence
followed Babylon, Nineveh, Venice,
London, haberdashers, goldsmiths,
taverns, playhouses, satires, epigrams,
puns – these all came in on the town
part and thither side of innocence.

Charles Lamb

Sir Jason Pym heard about the fire, as did everyone else in the West End of London. He strolled past the earl's house the next day and saw squads of workmen and servants already busy cleaning up the mess.

By gossiping to various aristocratic passers-by, he was able to learn that Clarissa and the Tribbles had been guests of the earl's, and that the earl and his family had been taken to reside with the Tribbles in

Holles Street.

He felt his luck was in. Some way and somehow, Clarissa had not discovered those papers. Now that Bella was in the same household, it should surely be easy to persuade her to get them for him.

Sir Jason's one chink in his selfish armour was to believe himself irresistible to women. Bella had sent him a pathetic little note the day before to say how much she missed him and how terribly harsh she thought the earl's behaviour was. She begged him to meet her in St James's Park at three o'clock tomorrow – now today. Blinded by vanity, Sir Jason did not realize that Bella was fickle and that she would probably have spurned him had not her brother's interference added a necessary spice of intrigue to the liaison.

He dressed in his dandified best, from high starched collar to gleaming boots and clouded cane, and waited in the park at the spot where the dairymaids sold fresh milk, which was where Bella had said she would meet him.

Promptly at three o'clock, he saw her hurrying towards him. He recognized her figure, for Bella, alive to the dramatics of the situation, was heavily veiled. Bella flicked a gloved hand at her maid to indicate the woman was to make herself scarce for a short while.

'I am glad you are safe,' said Sir Jason in what he prided himself was a voice throbbing with passion. 'I heard about the fire.'

Bella put back her veil. 'The most horrid thing,' she said. 'It was all the fault of that great lummox, Clarissa Vevian. She set her scarf alight and in doing so set the whole drawing room burning. Crispin then accused me and Mama of having deliberately engineered the fire so as to get the drawing room refurbished. He is a monster! He is not even in love with this Miss Vevian, for I observed them closely. He is sorry for her.'

'Why is he sorry for her, my heart?' asked Sir Jason. 'She is a very rich young lady of good family.'

'She is notoriously clumsy and endangers the life and limb of all who come near her. That is why she has been sent to the Tribbles for schooling. They are an odd frowsty couple, terribly old. Mama is to try to persuade Crispin to let us go to a hotel until the town house is ready. She will find it difficult, for he has employed builders and carpenters and decorators to work night and day and says he expects the house to be habitable again in a week.'

'My poor crushed blossom,' said Sir Jason huskily. 'Would I had the right to protect you. Would I could make you mine.'

Bella thought it was all very romantic. She fluttered her eyelashes at him and sighed. 'Alas, that can never be so.'

'My heart is breaking!' cried Sir Jason, putting a white hand to his enamelled brow.

Bella quite warmed to him. He was behaving just as he ought. 'Dear Sir Jason,' she said, allowing him to press her hand, 'I wish there was something I could do to alleviate your pain.'

'There is, my life, a trifling service it might be easy to perform for me.'

'And what is that, sir?'

'A servant of mine, a thief, had taken some of my belongings and was hiding out at an inn. Miss Vevian stopped at that inn on her road to London. The authorities came to search for my wicked servant and he hid my belongings in various rooms about the inn and made his escape. All things belonging to me were recovered except for a packet of love letters. I caught the fellow myself and got him to confess. He said he hid the letters in the bottom of Miss Vevian's jewel box.'

'Then you have only to ask her for them,' said Bella pettishly. Love letters, indeed.

Men in love with Bella were not supposed ever to have been in love with anyone else.

'I cannot trust her not to read them,' he said, 'but I can trust you' – which all went to show what a bad judge of character Sir Jason was when he thought some female was besotted with him.

'What are these love letters?' asked Bella.

'I had an indiscreet affair with a certain royal personage. She wrote me passionate letters. It would ruin her if they were found. The packet is stitched tightly closed. It is an oilskin packet.'

Bella looked at him with cold eyes. The nerve of the man. To drag her out to this dingy park – Bella had forgotten it was she who had suggested the meeting – and to tell her lies about letters from some royal person! They were probably from some tart like Harriet Wilson and he wanted to destroy them. To dare to ask *her* to get back his love letters when he was supposed to be in love with her!

She dropped her veil. 'I must go,' she said, turning away.

'But the letters?'

'I suggest you ask Miss Vevian for them yourself,' said Bella huffily. 'You had better not come near me again. Crispin would not like it.'

She summoned her maid and tripped off down one of the walks, leaving him glaring after her.

Sir Jason walked up and down the park for some time, fretting and fuming. Then he remembered his latest recruit and his face lightened. Young Lord Sandford was the answer. None but Sir Crispin knew how badly in debt the young man was. He was handsome, of good family, and had a charming manner. He had lazily said he would do anything at all for money. He should start to pay off his debts by dancing attendance on Clarissa.

Clarissa was searching in her jewel box for a set of clasps to give to Yvette to put on a dress. Her fingers touched the oilskin packet at the bottom, but it was a large packet that exactly fitted the bottom of the jewel box and so she thought it was some sort of padding her maid had put there.

Bella appeared in the doorway of Clarissa's bed-chamber. 'Found anything?' she asked.

'I am looking for some sapphire clasps,' said Clarissa. 'I think I must have left them at home.'

'I suppose you hide your love letters in

there,' teased Bella, moving into the room and looking down curiously at the contents of the box. 'There is nothing in here but jewellery,' said Clarissa. 'I am not fortunate enough to have love letters.'

'Were there ever any love letters in that box?' pursued Bella.

'There never were and there are certainly none here now. See for yourself,' said Clarissa crossly. She raked aside the jewels. The oilskin packet was black and so Bella thought she was seeing the bottom of the box.

'I was only funning,' she said. 'You should be grateful I am speaking to you at all, after the way you behaved.'

'Lord Greystone is convinced the fire was not due to my clumsiness,' said Clarissa.

'Well, he *would* say that, would he not?' said Bella, her eyes bright with malice. 'He always did have a penchant for lame ducks.'

'I am not a lame duck!' cried Clarissa.

'Oh, no? Then why are you with the Tribbles? In any case, Crispin has better fish to fry. He has taken Chloris Deveney and her mother driving.'

'Then I trust he enjoys a pleasant outing. Do go away, Lady Bella. You do not like me one bit, so don't waste my time by trying to goad me.'

'Tut, tut. Temper, temper. Chloris is divinely fair, is she not?'

Clarissa looked ready to throw something, so Bella nipped quickly from the room.

So that's that, thought Clarissa. He is fond of me as he would be fond of a stray dog. I wish this Season were over. Mama and Papa must come to terms with my spinsterdom.

Clarissa did not know that the ambitious widow, Mrs Deveney, had been promenading up and down Holles Street with Chloris until they saw the earl emerge. Mrs Deveney had begged him to drive them to Pall Mall, saying her carriage was being repaired.

She went down to the drawing room to see Amy and ask when her lessons, which had been cancelled for that day, were to be resumed.

Not only was Amy in the drawing room, but Effy, Mr Haddon, Mr Randolph ... and Lady Angela.

Angela was sitting in the middle of the sofa with a gentleman on either side. Mr Randolph was carding wool for her while Mr Haddon was pouring tea. Amy and Effy stood forgotten by the window.

Clarissa cast them a quick look of understanding sympathy and then went to stand in front of Angela. 'Lady Angela,' she said, 'you must not embarrass our poor guests by making them work.' She deftly lifted the wool from Mr Randolph's fingers. He rose and bowed and went to join Amy and Effy. 'And Mr Haddon. I am perfectly able to pour tea as well as to card,' said Clarissa.

In a fury, Angela watched Mr Haddon escape as well. Clarissa smiled at her sweetly. 'What a pretty shade of wool,' she said.

Angela was seething. She had quickly discovered that both Mr Haddon and Mr Randolph were rich nabobs and was determined to secure one or the other for herself. A doting husband would buy her all the fripperies that Crispin would not. Crispin had declared that he would choose the colours, curtains, and furnishings for the ruined drawing room himself. He had been acid, biting and humiliating about the fire. Angela shuddered when she remembered that row. Then there was the worry that Crispin might find Clarissa attractive. Clarissa made Angela feel dull and faded. There was just too much of Clarissa. Her fingers holding the wool were long and slim and white. Her bosom was generous, and her figure, tall and slim. Her generous mouth was too large for beauty but her eyes were fine and well-spaced. Admittedly she had a great amount of luxuriant hair, but it was *red* – most unfortunate for Clarissa, thought Angela, trying to comfort herself.

Angela turned her head and smiled at Mr Randolph. 'La, sir,' she said, 'I feel I should beg you to return to my side. Miss Vevian is such a great giant of a creature that I feel quite dwarfed.'

Mr Randolph had been talking to Effy. He broke off and said, 'You, like me, Lady Angela, envy people of height. How I long to be as tall as my friend, Haddon. He makes me feel an insignificant little dab of a fellow.'

'Height in a man is very well,' said Angela, 'but a great disadvantage in a woman.'

'We are trying to train Miss Vevian in correct social behaviour, Lady Angela,' said Amy. 'I fear if you go on like this, she will think veiled malice is the order of the day.'

'Well, really!' said Angela, leaping to her feet and knocking over the sugar bowl. 'Now look what you've done,' she snapped at Clarissa. 'Pick it up. I am going to my room and I shall tell Crispin on his return that I am not wanted here!'

She burst into tears. Mr Randolph made noises of distress and ran forward to comfort her. Amy got there first and put a firm arm around Angela's shoulders and urged her from the room.

Soon Angela was confiding her troubles to Bella. 'Those two old frumps will not let me get nigh one of their precious nabobs. Darling Bella, one of us must marry soon. Crispin holds the purse-strings much too tightly. You know my gown for the Pomfreys' ball? Well, I wanted to purchase fine lace for the edging, and do you know what Crispin said? He said I already had yards and yards of priceless lace and did not need to buy any more. Miser! But we must not make him angry again. You have not been seeing Sir Jason, have you?'

'No, Mama,' lied Bella. 'You know I told you I was tired of him. Let us hope we are out of here before the Pomfreys' ball, for that would mean we would have to go with the Tribbles and I do not want the stigma of being associated with them.'

'They are a couple of quizzes, dear, but terribly good *ton*.'

'But any *young* girl seen with them must be damned as one of their "impossibles". Do try to persuade Crispin to let us go to a hotel.'

Dinner that evening was an awkward meal.

The earl found himself wishing that just one other gentleman were present. He felt swamped by warring femininity. Angela was furious because he had refused point-blank to move to an hotel. Amy and Effy were jealous of Angela and feared she might succeed with Mr Haddon or Mr Randolph where they had failed, and Clarissa wished the earl would pay her more attention and not look so cross.

After dinner, the company agreed to go to bed early. Clarissa went down to the library to get a book. She was coming up the stairs again and past the drawing room when she heard Amy say, 'Miss Vevian is a thoroughly pleasant and attractive lady, Lord Greystone. Do you not think so?'

Heart beating hard, novel clutched to her bosom, Clarissa stood outside the door and listened for the earl's reply.

'Yes, she is a fine lady,' she heard the earl say, and her heart leaped with gladness. But then he added with a laugh, 'In fact, she is very like the sister I always hoped to have.'

Well, that was that. Clarissa's dreams crumbled. And that was all they had been, she thought – dreams. She would end her days being thought of as a 'good sort', like Amy Tribble, the sort of female to whom men confided their hopes and dreams of marrying someone else.

She felt very silly, sad, and disappointed, but, at the same time, strangely relieved. She would no longer need to tremble at the sound of his voice or scan his face in the hope of seeing some tenderness there. She was to go to the Pomfreys' ball. She had been excited, nervous, frightened, and elated at the prospect. Now she had nothing to worry about. It would be another evening to be endured, as she had endured so many in Bath.

But on the night of the ball itself, Clarissa found it almost impossible to remain calm. As she stepped out into Holles Street, the very air seemed to be charged with excitement. She knew her evening gown of white muslin decorated with a gold key pattern and cut in simple Grecian lines became her well. She had a wreath of artificial honeysuckle on her head and pretty gold sandals on her feet. The sky was paling to smoky blue behind the tall buildings and the air smelled of the ladies' perfumes. The earl's coachmen and footmen were in their best livery. The coach itself gleamed in the rays from the light above the door with its crested varnished panels and rich scarlet-and-gold hammer-cloth. In a house across the street, they were holding a musicale and a German tenor's voice, liquid and heart-breaking, came to their ears, singing of lost love. The London evening was warm and balmy, holding the promise of a splendid summer to come.

It was a night to dream of love and romance, and Clarissa dreamt of some young man who would be waiting at the ball, ready to fall in love with her. She had firmly come to terms with her feelings for the earl. She had been mistaken. One could not dream about or entertain yearning feelings for a man who thought of one as a sister. A little part of her treacherous mind noticed how very handsome, how very fine he looked in evening dress, but the rest of her brain concentrated firmly on the evening ahead.

They entered the carriage, all feeling a trifle cramped, although neither Mr Haddon nor Mr Randolph was of their party. Effy suffered most from the competition presented by Lady Angela. Until the arrival of Angela, Effy had been complacently proud of her fine silvery hair. But Angela's glossy-brown and youthful curls gave her a pang of pure envy.

Fear of cosmetic poisoning stopped Effy from wearing blanc, but no such fears had obviously entered Angela's mind. Even her bosom and arms were painted with white lead. Effy's gown had swathes of gauze filling in the neckline to disguise the sad sagging of ageing flesh. Angela's gown was cut low, exposing the top halves of two youthful-looking breasts. How does she do it? thought Effy, quite wretched with jealousy.

Amy's jealousy was not quite so intense. Still anxious to make up for the initial time lost in grooming Clarissa, she had spent all the time up to the ball in Clarissa's company, supervising her tutors and trying to train her to move slowly and gracefully at all times. Ever since the earl had said he thought Clarissa was like the sister he would have liked to have, Amy had decided he was a lost cause. No hope there at all. Outright dislike would have been easier to combat. There was nothing any woman could do about brotherly affection. To her relief, Clarissa did not appear to entertain any warm feelings towards the earl at all.

For his part, the earl was quiet and thoughtful on the road to the ball. The day before, he had called on the Prince Regent to pay his respects. The prince was in an affable mood and showed a desire to gossip. 'Has Your Royal Highness seen anything lately of Sir Jason Pym?' asked the earl at last.

The prince pouted, looking like a sulky child. 'We have not seen him this age.' He shifted restlessly. 'His demands for money began to embarrass us.'

'But he appears to be extremely wealthy now,' said the earl. 'And yet, as far as I recall, he was not granted any land with his knighthood.'

'We do not know how he gains his money, but we suspect it is at the card tables. Demme, Greystone,' said the prince, dropping the royal 'we', 'I am sure that fellow is a card sharp. Something vulgar about him. Sort of fellow who preys on the young and silly.'

The earl now turned the prince's words over in his mind. He had not had much opportunity since the fire to be on the look-out for possible spies. It also seemed an extraordinarily difficult task. He had only asked about Sir Jason because he feared Bella might be seeing the man on the sly and because he had wondered if he had been too harsh on Jason. After all, there was a lot of malicious gossip about other people who had found royal favour, most of it unfounded.

Could Sir Jason be one of those aristocratic spies the War Office was searching for? What was Sir Jason's background? Certainly not aristocratic. The earl cast his mind back to his Oxford days. Ah, he had it. Jason's father had been a successful furniture-maker who had social ambitions for his son. He had sent him to Oxford University in the hope the lad would make aristocratic connections rather than to further his education. Gossip again. But probably reliable. Might be worth looking the father up. His business was in Kensington, set somewhere among the nurseries that supplied London with fruit and vegetables.

The carriage jolted to a halt and the earl returned to the present. He was glad Bella and Angela had given up being spiteful about Clarissa. Repairs to the drawing room were going on so quickly that they should be able to return to the town house in a few days.

The Pomfreys had packed in as many people as they could. The edges of the ballroom were crowded with people standing and gossiping.

The earl, like the Tribbles, hoped Clarissa

would have at least a moderate success. Like them, he watched anxiously as a young captain led her onto the floor where the set for a Scottish reel was being made up.

At first Clarissa danced very well, moving easily through the intricacies of the reel. He caught her eye and smiled. Clarissa bumped into the person next to her with such force that the man nearly fell over. From then on, she repeatedly lost her place, trod on people's toes, and was in a state of abject misery by the time the reel finished.

'Have you ever seen such a clumsy girl?' crowed Angela to Bella. 'Who is going to dance with her now?'

'Look!' hissed Bella. 'Who is that divinely handsome man who has approached her?'

Angela looked across the ballroom in surprise. A young man, only about an inch shorter than Clarissa, had gone up to her. He had thick brown hair arranged in The Windswept and deep blue eyes in a fine aristocratic face. His figure was excellent.

Bella's next partner came up to claim her and Angela slipped off to find out the identity of Clarissa's new partner.

'I am Sandford,' the young man was saying. 'Lord George Sandford, and you are the Honourable Clarissa Vevian.'

'How do you know my name?' asked Clarissa.

'I made it my business to find out.'

Clarissa sighed. 'After my disgraceful performance in the Scottish reel, I am sure everyone made it their business to find out. I cannot dance with you, sir. I am too nervous and will forget the steps.'

'It is the waltz. I will guide you. Come, Miss Vevian. You know what they say when you fall off a horse? You must get up immediately and try again.'

Clarissa laughed. 'Just for a little,' she said. 'But you may return me to my seat if I prove too difficult a partner. First, I must ask the permission of my chaperones.'

She turned towards where Amy and Effy were sitting and both nodded their approval at the same time.

'Although he should have asked us first, don't you think?' said Amy.

'It's youth,' sighed Effy. 'So gay, so impetuous!'

'You really have been neglecting your duties,' said Amy crossly. 'We are both supposed to be chaperones. We will need to find some way to stop Clarissa from mangling her partners. Oh, no! I cannot bear it! There she goes again!'

Clarissa had just trodden on Lord Sandford's toes. He winced. 'You see? said Clarissa miserably. 'It is impossible. *I* am impossible. You may retire, my lord.'

He pressed his hand more firmly against her waist. 'If only you knew how much like a Greek goddess you look, Miss Vevian, then you would behave like one.'

'Come, my lord, you are teasing me.'

'Not I. That is why I immediately asked who you were. Your hair is like dark fire and your eyes like silver.'

'You can take your hands away from your eyes,' said Effy. 'She is dancing very prettily.'

Amy peeked through her fingers and then slowly lowered her hands. 'Well, I declare it's a miracle,' she said. 'She looks quite a different creature. And what a divine-looking man. And young! Greystone was too old for her anyway.'

Effy sighed. 'Ah, I can remember when the young men used to look at me in just the same way as Lord Sandford is looking at Clarissa.'

'Really?' said Amy waspishly. 'How odd that none of them ever asked you to dance.'

'Oh, your poor old addled brain,' said Effy. 'You have been having quite frightening lapses of memory of late. Still, it is only to

150

be expected.'

'We are twins and therefore of the same age, or had you forgot?'

'La, no! But I have noticed that unfeminine women age much more quickly than ladies who take care of themselves.'

'If being feminine means covering your face with mud of a night and tying up your chin so that you look like a Gothic fright, then I am glad I am not feminine. Nothing more sad than a faded beauty – nothing more dreadfully sad than a faded woman who thinks she has any claim to beauty.'

'I could strike you dead!' hissed Effy, raising her fan.

Amy put up her fists. 'Just you try!' she jeered.

'Ladies,' came Clarissa's voice. 'Lord Sandford wishes to escort me to the supper room.'

The two raging Tribbles immediately pinned smiles on their faces. 'Of course, my dear,' cooed Effy.

'What are we fighting about?' demanded Amy when the couple had walked off. 'Look here, Effy, we should be supporting each other. That vulgar trollop Angela is about to thieve one of our nabobs.'

'What chance has she?'

'Every chance. She is a titled lady and

comparatively well-looking for her age. If we continue to fight, then she will sneak off with one of 'em when we're not looking. She may even be seeing one of them on the quiet now.'

'They are both much too sensible to be taken in by such a creature.'

'We both know gentlemen like addle-pated clinging women,' said Amy. 'Truce, Effy. We must plan how to trounce her.'

Effy looked gloomily to where Angela, instead of sitting among the chaperones like themselves, was dancing with a well-preserved colonel. 'Truce,' she said in a hollow voice.

Clarissa was behaving very well in the supper room. Greek goddesses do not drop things. That compliment gave her poise. She asked Lord Sandford a great many questions about himself and was content to listen. Lord Sandford thought his mission was going to be much easier and pleasanter than he had expected. He told her about a famous race he had taken part in to Box Hill and how he had won. He told her how Gentleman Jackson himself had praised his prowess in boxing. Clarissa listened with rapt attention to all this bragging, for he managed to talk with a sort of engaging self-deprecation as if perpetually ruefully surprised at his own success. His blue eyes gazed warmly into Clarissa's and she felt relaxed and happy.

The Earl of Greystone had meant to dance at least one dance with Clarissa. But Sir Jason was present and in the card room. The earl followed him there to study what he did and whom he spoke to. There appeared to be nothing sinister about Sir Jason. He was foppish and conceited but hardly the type of man who would murder a widow on Brighton beach or risk being hanged for treason.

The earl then spoke to him civilly. Sir Jason replied pleasantly, unexpected behaviour from a man who had been warned off such a short time ago.

They played a hand of piquet. The earl won. He had a feeling he had been allowed to win, but then dismissed it as nonsense. He and Sir Jason returned to the ballroom together. Clarissa was once more dancing with Lord Sandford. She looked radiant and very young. They both looked very young, thought the earl.

'I see Miss Vevian is dancing with Lord Sandford. Another success for the Tribbles if they pull that off,' drawled Sir Jason. 'Lots of money and a fine sportsman.'

'A friend of yours?' asked the earl, his eyes on Clarissa.

'No, a mere acquaintance, I assure you.'

The earl bowed and left him and made his way around the edge of the ballroom to join Angela. A group of people blocked his way. He hesitated, and then turned and looked once more at Clarissa, and as he looked, she pirouetted under Lord Sandford's arm, and then he could swear Lord Sandford looked across her to where someone was standing and winked. The earl craned his head; Sir Jason was still standing at the entrance to the card room and it was in that direction that Lord Sandford had winked.

The group blocking his way dispersed and instead of joining Angela, he went to sit next to the Tribble sisters.

'Miss Vevian appears to be enjoying herself,' he said casually.

'Oh, she is very popular,' said Effy complacently. 'Lord Sandford is quite smitten with her.'

'I must ask her to spare me a dance,' he said.

'She can't,' said Effy triumphantly. 'Every space in her card is taken up for the rest of the evening.'

'Good, good,' said the earl, and immediately felt old and pompous and stuffy.

Something about his manner prompted Amy to say, 'I know you have a *brotherly* affection for Miss Vevian, and so you, too, must be delighted at her success. And Lord Sandford! Such a personable young man, don't you think?'

'Yes, yes,' he said, suddenly highly irritated. 'But go carefully, ladies. What do you really know of this Lord Sandford?

'Only that he is rich and young and very, very handsome,' said Amy.

The earl got to his feet and bowed. 'I don't know why I come to these affairs,' he said crossly. 'Cursed flat.'

'Now that was *very* rude of him,' said Effy, her eyes round.

'Ye-e-e-s. Wasn't it just?' said Amy, watching the earl move away. 'Now, I wonder...'

6

Let us drink and be merry, dance, joke, and
* rejoice,*
With claret and sherry, theorbo and voice!
The changeable world to our joy is unjust,
A treasure's uncertain, then down with your
* dust;*
In frolics dispose your pounds, shillings and
* pence,*
For we shall be nothing a hundred years hence.

Thomas Jordan

The earl rode out the next day to search for Jason's father in Kensington. He should really have been paying a call on Chloris Deveney, the only lady he had danced with at the ball, but had sent his servant instead to present his compliments. How awkward it had been dancing with Chloris. He should not have asked her to waltz. She was so very small and dainty and yet he had not felt protective or manly in the least. She had talked a great deal and he had had to bend his head to catch what she was saying. Unlike Clarissa. But he hadn't danced with Clarissa. Hadn't had the opportunity. But he would have been able to look into her eyes and hear every word she said. He would have been able to confide his worries about Bella and Angela to her.

But at least Clarissa was happy now. She had her beau. She had written to her father to ask for money to buy the Tribbles a new drawing-room carpet. The viscount, grateful that his daughter did not seem to have committed any major follies, because the earl had taken full responsibility for the disaster to the coach, had sent a generous sum and Clarissa had ordered a very fine blue-and-rose Chinese carpet which had been delivered that very day while she was entertaining Lord Sandford. Amy and Effy had been thrilled and Lord Sandford had joined in the fun of helping Clarissa and the servants roll up the old damaged carpet and put down the new one.

If only he could forget that wink. If Lord Sandford had winked at Sir Jason – why?

The day was warm and gusty and the air of Kensington was scented with blossom. He asked at an inn for the whereabouts of a furniture-maker called Pym and was directed to an address near Kensington Gardens.

The furniture-maker's manufactory was quite big. It had been an old farm, and now the buildings surrounding what used to be the farmyard had been converted into workshops.

He dismounted and presented his card to one of the workmen and asked for Mr Pym.

He had been expecting to meet an older version of Sir Jason, so it was with some surprise that he found himself confronted by a rotund little man wearing an old-fashioned wig and a baize apron over working clothes.

'And what can I do for you, my lord?' demanded Mr Pym eagerly.

'I was thinking of buying some pieces of furniture,' said the earl cautiously.

'This way, this way, my lord,' said Mr Pym, bowing low and then leading the way into one of the buildings. The earl looked at the furniture. It was very good, he noted with surprise, light and delicate in the latest mode. He needed furniture for the drawing room, and so he might as well order it from Mr Pym. The prices were reasonable, too. For a brief fleeting moment he wished Clarissa were with him to choose the colours for the upholstery. Mr Pym then begged his lordship to step into the office for a glass of wine.

The earl turned the glass in his long fingers

and then said, 'I think I know your son, Mr Pym – Sir Jason.'

The jovial little man's face grew hard, but he said politely, 'Sir Jason is indeed my son.'

'You must be very proud of him,' said the earl.

'Why?' asked the furniture-maker sharply.

'He is a knight and has been a friend of the Prince Regent.'

'And full of a great deal of nonsense and folly,' said Mr Pym. 'Oh, it is all my own fault, my lord. I wanted him to go to Oxford and meet the grand folk and so have a good connection for the trade. I am old now and he was to succeed me. He not only refused to have anything to do with the business, he told his grand friends I was dead. He told lies about me, about his upbringing. I finally refused to give him a penny, hoping that would bring him to his senses. He robbed me while I was asleep and then disappeared. I could not go to the authorities, I could not see my own son hang. Then I heard he had found royal favour. The Prince Regent must have given him great sums of money, for I gather from my spies he has been living in a very grand style for quite some time.'

'I am sorry,' said the earl. 'It must have been a sad blow to you.'

Mr Pym sighed. 'I do very well now. I have built up a fine business. But it breaks a man's heart not to have a son to leave it to.'

The earl and Mr Pym talked for some time, Mr Pym promising to have the furniture delivered. Then the earl rode off, deep in thought. Surely here was the type of man he was supposed to be looking for, someone who had a great deal of money and yet no visible means of support. As he rode past Kensington Gardens, he would have been surprised to know that the subject of his thoughts was quite close, strolling in Kensington Gardens, waiting for Mrs Loomis, the Tribbles' housekeeper.

Sir Jason had previously managed to strike up an acquaintance with the housekeeper. It was she who had tried to get the packet from Clarissa's jewel box for Sir Jason. She knew Sir Jason as Mr Kennedy, a respectable merchant. She was not a bad woman, nor had he bribed her, but he had said he was a widower and had hinted he was looking for a wife. Mrs Loomis was a spinster – as was the case with most housekeepers, the 'Mrs' was a courtesy title.

After her failure to retrieve the letters for him, she had felt so guilty and been so frightened that she had begged him not to ask her to do such a thing again, and so he had been forced to recruit Sandford.

Then she had sent him a note to a perfumer's in the Haymarket where he sometimes collected letters addressed to the fictitious Mr Kennedy, as he used that name for various other schemes.

He did not want to see her, but was afraid that if he did not, she would speak to the Tribbles about him. Certainly they would never connect Sir Jason Pym with the Mr Kennedy she would talk about. He wore his hair unpowdered, had put wax pads in his cheeks to alter the shape of his face, and his clothes were sober and correct. To complete the disguise, he wore a pair of green-tinted spectacles.

Mrs Loomis came hurrying up to him. She was a small, fat woman, scarlet in the face with the effort of hurrying.

'Oh, Mr Kennedy,' she gasped. 'I'm that glad to see you.'

'Gently, my dear, Mrs Loomis, gently, I pray you.'

'It's that Harris, the butler. Everyone else thinks Miss was having a bad dream when she surprised me in her room, but Harris, he wrote again to my previous employer to check my reference again and he looks at me in such a way.'

Sir Jason reflected sourly that butlers and housekeepers were usually at loggerheads and that the efficient Harris had probably rechecked the other servants' references as well.

'I am sure it is all your imagination,' he said soothingly.

'What I wanted to ask,' said Mrs Loomis, 'is if you wouldn't mind me telling Mr Harris about them letters. It's innocent enough. I'll just tell him what you told me.'

'No!' said Sir Jason fiercely. 'Look, Mrs Loomis, as housekeeper, surely you have ample opportunity to go into the girl's room. It would only take a minute.'

'I daren't risk it, Mr Kennedy,' said Mrs Loomis. 'When Miss is out, her maid is usually in her room, sewing or checking things. No, trust me, Mr Kennedy, honesty is my motto. Much better to make a clean breast of things.'

They walked in the direction of Hyde Park, Mrs Loomis arguing and Sir Jason protesting.

He hoped to get her to swear to keep quiet, but the more he tried, the more stubborn Mrs Loomis became. If only Sir Jason had remembered to hold out those delicately hinted promises of marriage, then things might have gone his way. But as the housekeeper argued, gradually Sir Jason dropped his role of Mr Kennedy and became more arrogant and bad tempered.

'Pray sit down for a moment, my dear Mrs Loomis,' he said, all but thrusting her down on an iron park bench.

'I've made up my mind, honesty is the best policy,' said Mrs Loomis for what was – or so it seemed to Sir Jason – the hundredth time. 'Only see how my poor heart beats.'

She put a chubby gloved hand to her bosom.

'So it does,' marvelled Sir Jason. 'Good gracious. I can see it beating from here.'

'You can?' Mrs Loomis removed her hand and stared down at her own bosom in awe.

Sir Jason drew a flask from his pocket. 'Quickly, a good mouthful of brandy, Mrs Loomis, to restore you.'

Gratefully, the housekeeper took a hearty swig. She began to talk again about her honesty and her good character and Sir Jason patiently listened while the heavy dose of chloral she had just taken mixed in the brandy began to take effect. In no time at all, she was unconscious and snoring horribly.

He looked quickly about. There were plenty of people in the Park but no one near the bench on which they sat. He drew a long thin knife from one capacious pocket and gently eased it out of its sheath. Another quick look around and then he struck like a snake, driving the thin point of the knife into the housekeeper's heart.

He pressed her body firmly into the support of the arm rest so that she would look as if she were asleep. He draped a fold of her stole over the handle of the knife. It was a good knife but he would need to leave it. If he pulled it out, then blood would spurt all over the place.

He got to his feet and walked quietly away.

Stupid woman, he thought.

Angela was delighted to find herself alone in the drawing room with Mr Haddon later that day. He smiled at her and said the ladies had gone upstairs to change. Angela got to work. She flattered him, she flirted with him, but he remained polite and a trifle distant.

Angela hated the Tribble sisters. They must have poisoned this man's mind against her. They had no hope themselves and so they were determined that no one else should have any hope either. If only she could give them a fright.

It was when she heard them moving about upstairs, making sounds preparatory to coming downstairs, that she hit on a plan.

She waited until she heard the footsteps move to the landing above and acted quickly. 'Oh, Mr Haddon,' she cried, 'I have dropped my diamond pin. My eyes are not very good and that new carpet is so thick. Can you see if it is under my chair?'

Mr Haddon stood up and bent down and looked under her chair. 'I am sure I can see it,' said Angela. 'There!'

Looking puzzled, Mr Haddon got down on his knees. Effy and Amy appeared in the doorway.

'Oh, Mr Haddon,' breathed Angela. Still kneeling, he looked into her face in some surprise. She took his hand in both of hers and smiled at him mistily.

To the Tribble sisters it looked as if Mr Haddon had just proposed and had been accepted.

Amy turned and ran up the stairs. Priding herself she was made of stronger stuff, Effy went into the room, only to hear, to her amazement, Mr Haddon saying very crossly as he snatched his hand away, 'I cannot find your diamond pin anywhere under your chair, Lady Angela.' He got to his feet and bowed to Effy. 'You seem to have been away a very long time.'

'Mr Haddon and I have been sharing secrets,' giggled Angela.

'No, my lady, we have not,' said Mr Haddon, looking at Effy's distressed face.

And then Amy erupted into the drawing room like a fury.

The Earl of Greystone let himself into the house in Holles Street. As he mounted the stairs, he wondered if there had been a death in the house, it was so hushed and quiet. A housemaid cast him a scared look and backed against the wall of the stairs to let him past.

He went into the drawing room. There was only Clarissa there, sitting on the sofa, reading.

'Where is everyone?' he asked.

Clarissa put down her book. 'The most frightful scene has taken place, my lord. Miss Amy is in disgrace and Lady Angela has just left off having hysterics.'

'What on earth has happened?'

'It appears that when Miss Effy and Miss Amy entered the drawing room earlier, they found Mr Haddon on his knees in front of Lady Angela. They assumed he was proposing marriage. It transpired that Lady Angela had told Mr Haddon she had dropped a diamond pin under her chair and I think – if you will forgive me, my lord – she contrived to make it look as if Mr Haddon was proposing so as to bait the Tribbles. It worked only too well.'

'Were the sisters very distressed?'

'Effy seemed to be coping quite well, or so I gathered from a rather stunned Mr Haddon who told me about it. But Amy, as soon as she saw what she thought was a proposal to Lady Angela, ran up the stairs and then came back. She snatched Lady Angela's hair from her head, revealing it was only a wig, and poor Lady Angela is nearly bald under it. But there was worse.'

'There can't be,' said the earl faintly.

'Miss Amy threw a pair of false breasts which she had got from Lady Angela's room on the floor in front of Mr Haddon and shouted, "Try running your hands over these, Mr Haddon, for that is what you will find in your marriage bed!"'

Clarissa began to laugh helplessly. The earl began to laugh as well and soon they were both holding on to each other. As their laughter finally died away, Clarissa looked at the earl in a startled way and moved along the sofa.

'I have had so many adventures since I left home,' she said. 'First I set a coach on fire, then I nearly kill a man...'

'Tom was only winded.'

'No, not Tom. I have not told you before because ... well, because it was all rather frightening and I never found out how he had fared. After I left your home, we put up at The Bell, where your servant had ordered a room – that is, I and my maid. My poor maid became tipsy at the dinner table and this rabbity young man offered to help me up the stairs with her. I gave him the key to my room to go ahead and open the door, but when he came back to me, I noticed his lavender gloves were streaked with black and I immediately knew he had been in my jewel box because everything was black from the fire. I struck out at him. He fell down the stairs and was knocked out just as the redcoats arrived, the ones who were searching for those missing government papers. I did not tell the colonel he was a thief because I was afraid he might hang and he had not had time to take anything, but I do hope he recovered from his fall.'

'That's odd,' said the earl slowly. 'That must have been around the time that someone broke into my home and ransacked Bella's and Angela's rooms. Dear girl, is it possible that instead of taking something out of your jewel box, he put something in, like those missing papers?'

'No, there is nothing there. I looked.'

'Perhaps I had better go to The Bell and see what I can find out.' Sir Jason, thought the earl. Sir Jason, who had oiled his way in after the attempted robbery, asking questions about a 'member of his family' who had been staying at The Bell.

He got up and smiled down at Clarissa. 'In the meantime, Angela may have her wish. She and Bella will be removed to a hotel tonight.' Clarissa got to her feet as well. Sandford, thought the earl suddenly. He had winked at Jason when he was dancing with Clarissa, or that is what it had looked like.

He took both her hands in his. 'Promise me one thing,' he said.

'Yes?'

'If, while I am gone, Lord Sandford proposes marriage, please do not accept until I return.'

'You are not my father,' said Clarissa huffily. 'I shall do as I please.'

170

Amy came into the room. The earl released Clarissa's hands. Clarissa, assuming Amy would want to apologize to him in private, curtsied and left the room.

To Amy's relief, the earl seemed more amused than angry. He gracefully accepted her apologies and told her that he was going upstairs to ask Bella and Angela to make ready to leave.

'I am going to the country tomorrow,' he said to Amy. 'I have a favour to ask you. If Lord Sandford proposes marriage to Clarissa, do not let Clarissa accept the proposal until I return.'

'Nothing to do with you,' said Amy roundly. She sniffed. 'You and your brotherly love! Since Clarissa met that young man at the ball last night, she has not dropped anything. The admiration of a handsome man is just what she needs. As a matter of fact,' said Amy airily, but watching the earl closely, 'Sandford was sounding me out today, you know, to find out how the land lies and if you entertained any warm feelings towards Clarissa. "Not a bit of it," said I. "Looks on her as a sister." "How can it be," says he to me, "that any man in his right mind can share the same roof as Clarissa Vevian and look on her as a sister?" "Gentlemen," says I, "gets

171

staid and sober when they are as old as the Earl of Greystone." Amy finished, feeling quite exhausted at having delivered herself of so many lies in such a short space of time.

'And did Miss Vevian *also* go out of her way to tell you about her sisterly feelings towards *me?*' demanded the earl acidly.

'Oh, no. Mind you, there was a time when I hoped...'

'You hoped what?'

'Oh, nothing,' said Amy. 'Young Sandford is just what she needs. He tells her she's beautiful almost in every second breath and it works with Clarissa like magic. Why, it's like seeing a clumsy, rusty piece of machinery being oiled and put into good working order. She presided over the tea table while he was here and you have never seen such dexterity and grace! Love has done what neither we nor her tutors could achieve.'

'I have reasons for asking you to be wary of Sandford,' said the earl.

'I suppose you must have good reasons,' said Amy. 'Not as if a man of your years could be jealous.'

'Dammit! I am thirty-two.'

'Pity,' said the incorrigible Amy, shaking her head. 'But there's none of us can turn back the clock.'

'Good evening, madam,' said the earl frostily. He marched up the stairs to tell Angela the good news about moving to a hotel. But instead of going to Angela's room, he went straight into Clarissa's without even bothering to knock. She was sitting at her toilet table, brushing her hair, which cascaded like a gleaming red waterfall down to her waist.

He stood behind her and put his hands on her shoulders and studied her reflection in the glass. 'Don't do anything to encourage Sandford until I get back,' he said.

'Why?' demanded Clarissa.

His grip on her shoulders tightened. 'Because I say so, Miss Vevian. Because I...'

She stared at the glass and saw his mouth descend to her cheek. She sat very still. 'Do this for me,' he said huskily.

'But I like him,' whispered Clarissa. 'He makes me feel pretty.'

His hands moved from her shoulders and buried themselves in the perfumed masses of her hair. He thought of Sandford kissing her and suddenly could not bear it. His head moved round, blotting out Clarissa's wide-eyed reflection in the glass and his lips found hers. His mouth was hard and firm and then soft and caressing. She twisted around in his arms and put her own arms around his neck.

Amy stood in the open doorway and surveyed the embrace with deep satisfaction. Then she crept off along the passage, rubbing her hands gleefully.

Effy listened breathlessly while Amy told her what had happened.

'But he might go too far,' she cried. 'We had better go and see what is going on. His intentions may be totally dishonourable, for all we know.'

'Spoilsport, leave 'em alone,' said Amy with a grin. 'The door's open.'

'Now, kiss me properly,' the Earl of Greystone was saying as he closed Clarissa's bedroom door and locked it. She walked back into his arms and he held her closely for a long moment and then began to kiss her passionately. He lifted her in his arms, and, still kissing her, carried her to the bed and laid her down on it and stretched out beside her.

His lips moved to her neck and then slowly down to the top of her breasts. 'He hasn't said anything about loving you,' said a high, clear voice somewhere inside Clarissa's brain. One hand slid round her back and loosened the tapes of her gown. Then he pulled down her gown and began to kiss her breasts.

'Clarissa! Open this door immediately.' Amy's voice, high and angry. She had been urged back by Effy and had been shocked to find the door shut.

The earl pulled up Clarissa's gown and retied the tapes and then helped her from the bed. Clarissa stood, her hair tumbled about her shoulders, looking the very picture of shame.

'Don't let any man near you when I am gone,' he whispered fiercely. 'Not even Sandford, especially Sandford. You are mine, and I love you.'

Clarissa's head came up and her eyes blazed with a mixture of love and relief. The Earl of Greystone unlocked the door.

'Ladies,' he said, 'I wish to ask your permission to pay my addresses to Miss Clarissa Vevian.'

'Looks like you have already been paying very warm addresses, my lord,' said Amy, peering over his shoulder. 'Yes, of course you may.'

Lady Angela was in a bad mood. She and Bella had longed to get away from the Tribbles and into a fashionable hotel. So here they were and they were not happy one bit. The Tribbles' household was very well run, the servants were deferential, and the food was excellent. Johnson's Hotel catered for the nobility, but employed all the sharp practices of the lower order of London hotels. You picked up a vase and it came apart in your hands, because it had been cunningly glued to do just that. You rang for another vase and they promptly supplied it and put the price of it on your bill. Rabbit was served up under a heavy sauce and called chicken and a great many other dishes had long and fancy French names to add tone to the mess they actually were. Angela's chamber-pot had fallen into two halves at a crucial moment.

It was not the discomforts of hotel life, which they had brought on themselves, that was so galling, nor the humiliating scene with Amy; it was the feeling that the earl and Clarissa were up to something. There had been a great air of excitement about the house when they left. Angela had never seen Crispin look so elated or so happy, and those wretched Tribbles had looked triumphant.

'She can't have lured Greystone into marriage, can she?' wailed Angela. 'A big giantess like that will probably breed and breed, and there'll be nothing left for poor Tom or Peregrine.'

'Not to mention me,' said Bella acidly.

'She seemed set on Sandford only the other day,' wailed Angela. 'Though how Sandford could even look at her with you in the room, Bella, I do not know.'

'I think,' said Bella slowly, 'that Sandford has proposed and been accepted. That is why those horrible Tribbles were looking so pleased with themselves. Clarissa is to be at the Herveys' breakfast this afternoon. We will be able to observe her there.'

'Sandford only met her for the first time at the ball. He can't have proposed. It must be Crispin.'

'Come, Mama, he would surely have told us.'

'No, he wouldn't; nasty, secretive thing,' said Angela. 'Let us see if there is some way we can shame her at the breakfast. It would get back to Cnspin's ears and might give him a disgust of her.'

Lord Sandford looked up rather guiltily as he found Sir Jason looming over him in the coffee room of the club to which they both belonged.

'Well, Sandford?' demanded Sir Jason.

'Where are the papers?'

'You are rushing me,' said Lord Sandford. 'I cannot just say to a girl I danced with only a short time ago, "Take me up to your bedroom and let me see your jewel box."'

'Where is your fire and passion, man? Tell her they are love letters stolen from you and you must have them back. I told you what to say. Time is running out. Do you want money or don't you? One word from me, and all the duns and debtors will be on your father's doorstep.'

'Why are you threatening me?' asked Lord Sandford plaintively. 'I thought all this was a lark. I mean, no one in their right mind would want to help Boney. If I thought for a minute he had one hope, I would have nothing to do with it.'

Sir Jason sat down and hitched his chair close. 'She goes to the Herveys' breakfast. Be there. Promise her marriage, promise her anything, but get those papers or it will be the worse for you.'

Lord Sandford recoiled from the vicious painted face thrust so close to his own. 'I say,' he said weakly. 'No need to turn nasty. I'll get them. She's already eating out of my hand.'

7

For if my libations exceed three,
I feel my heart becomes so sympathetic,
That I must have recourse to black Bohee;
'Tis pity wine should be so deleterious,
For tea and coffee leave us much more serious.

Lord Byron

As the earl rode out early the next morning, he was still amazed that he had had the good sense to find out he was in love with Clarissa.

He had been prepared to see her marry someone else, had looked on her with affection and admiration, and then Amy had goaded him. A smile curved his lips. He wondered now if Amy had goaded him deliberately. Was that part of their job? To jog the minds and affections of their 'impossibles" suitors? Perhaps if he had left things one more day, Sandford might have proposed and Clarissa might have accepted.

Sandford! He spurred his horse. It would probably turn out that Sir Jason made his money cardsharping and that Sandford was a respectable young man.

His thoughts turned again to Clarissa. He wished now he had exercised more control in his lovemaking. She was a virgin but she had answered his kisses with such passion that he had forgotten himself. He almost turned on the road at that point and headed straight back to London. For the thought came into his mind that surely his happiness with Clarissa mattered more than hunting down spies. But telling himself he was being downright unpatriotic and sending up a prayer for Clarissa's safety while he was gone, he bent over the horse's neck and rode like the wind.

When he reached The Bell he was weary from the journey, weary of changing horses, aching to see Clarissa again with a longing that was so sharp it was close to pain.

He ordered a room and then asked the waiter to send the landlord up to see him.

The landlord came in, wiping his hands on his apron, and looking anxiously at the earl. 'I trust everything is to your liking, my lord?

'Yes, splendid. Come here, man, I wish to ask you a few questions, that is all.'

The landlord walked forward and stood at attention. The earl looked at him with some amusement 'An old army man?'

'Yes, my lord, Twenty-sixth Foot.'

'How long since you left?'

'Ten years, my lord. I was in India with Wellington's troops. Got enough prize money to buy this inn.'

'And your name?'

'Sam Budgee, my lord.'

'Well, Mr Budgee, this is what I want to know. You may remember that I paid for a room for a young lady some time ago. She stayed here on the night the troops were searching for those missing government papers.'

'I remember that evening well, my lord.'

'You may also recall a certain young man who had an accident He fell down the stairs, I believe.'

'A Mr Epsom. Yes, my lord.'

The earl searched his memory. Epsom. Then he remembered during one of his leaves meeting a certain Mr Epsom at Watier's. A weak, rabbity-looking fellow who gambled deep.

'Did he recover from his fall?'

'Seems he did, my lord, although I thought it folly for him to go on the road so soon after recovering consciousness; but a gentleman came for him and bore him off.'

'This gentleman, what did he look like?'

'I ain't one for describing people proper, my lord. Very much the aristocrat, begging your parding. Very grand and haughty-like.'

'Hair? Colouring?'

'His hair was powdered white and worn long in the old-fashioned way. He had black eyes and his face was painted white. He had a coat of some light-blue cloth.'

'I know the gentleman of whom you speak,' said the earl. 'When they left here, which way did they go?'

'Out towards Bath, or so the ostlers told me'

'Thank you, Mr Budgee, that will be all.' Money changed hands and the landlord beamed and bowed.

'Will I set dinner for you now, my lord?'

'Not yet. Have a horse saddled and ready for me. I want to ride out for a little.'

Soon he was riding out on the Bath road. He had taken a description of Sir Jason's carriage. He planned to ask at houses on the Bath road if anyone had noticed the occupants of the carriage or had heard what they said. He had not much hope of success, but he was not hungry and felt spurred to take some sort of action.

The gibbet stood up beside the road in the

fading light. Normally, he would have averted his eyes from the poor wretches, but something made him look up as he rode underneath. He gave a sharp exclamation and reined in his horse. Three bodies were stinking and rotting. One at the end was also beginning to decay but the contorted face was vaguely familiar. The rain had washed it clean. He was sure it was Epsom.

He rode a little way away from the gibbet, his handkerchief over his nose and mouth so as not to breathe in the sickeningly sweet smell of rotting flesh.

If that body was Epsom's, then why was he up on that gibbet? He had left with Sir Jason, and Clarissa had not charged him with any crime.

Then a sinister little voice in his brain said, 'What a wonderful place to hide a body.'

He rode back to the inn and sent for the local magistrate.

Breakfasts were always held at three in the afternoon and the one Clarissa attended was no exception. The day was once more fine, unusual considering the customary fickleness of the English spring. The Herveys lived in a pleasant mansion overlooking the Green Park and the tables had been set on a long terrace outside in the open air.

Amy was looking very fine in a short spencer worn over a gown of green-and-white stripes. Effy was in pale blue muslin, her shoulders swathed in her favourite' blue gauze and a wide-brimmed bonnet decorated with silk roses and marguerites on her head. Clarissa was in pale green muslin with a green silk pelisse. Her straw hat was in the shape of a man's curly-brimmed beaver with the crown decorated with a broad green silk ribbon, the long ends, or streamers, hanging down her back.

She would have been enjoying herself immensely had not her partner at the table been Lord Sandford. Clarissa could think only of the earl. For the first time, she found Lord Sandford a trifle boring and thought that he bragged too much. She resented his proprietorial air but having encouraged him just the day before did not know how to go about repressing him.

His many compliments, which had done so much for her self-esteem before, now made her feel awkward and embarrassed. She dropped her fork, and when a waiter brought her another one, she dropped that as well. Lord Sandford was drinking heavily, Clarissa noticed, and his eyes shone with a hectic light.

From her watching post, farther down the table, Amy noticed Clarissa's confusion. Lord Sandford must be told as soon as possible that Clarissa was spoken for. Why didn't the girl tell him herself? She obviously had not, for he was constantly leaning towards her and whispering in her ear and totally ignoring the lady on his other side. Amy also noticed that Bella and Angela were watching Clarissa and exchanging occasional looks. They were plotting something, of that Amy was sure. Some way, she must put them out of action.

At last the meal came to an end and the guests were invited to take a stroll in the long gardens, which ran down to the park below the terrace

Amy seized Effy and drew her aside. 'I must deal with Sandford,' she whispered. 'But Bella and Angela are plotting mischief. While I cope with Sandford, you make sure they don't get near her.'

'What shall we do?' Bella was asking her mother eagerly, and they moved to the head of the steps among the other guests who were anxious to see the gardens.

'I have been thinking,' said Angela. 'Do you mark that goldfish pond? If we could cause her to fall in, then she would have to leave the party, and you, my love, could try your wiles on Sandford. She would look like such a fool and Crispin would get to hear of it.'

'She is with Sandford just now,' whispered Bella. 'How do we get near her?'

'We'll follow them and look for an opportunity.'

They were unaware that Effy was standing behind them, listening to every word.

Effy looked at the back of Angela's head, her eyes burning with hate. She followed them to the top of the stairs and seized her parasol. She was about to drive it into Angela's back, therefore causing her to take a tumble, but common sense stopped her at the last minute. The flight of steps was short and Angela would only fall onto the springy turf, pick herself up and be ready for action.

Angela and Bella moved down into the gardens and Effy followed them closely.

Amy came up to where Lord Sandford was standing with Clarissa beside the goldfish pond and hailed him cheerfully. 'Pleasant afternoon, Sandford.'

Lord Sandford turned, quickly hiding his irritation at the intrusion, and bowed. 'I have been telling Miss Vevian her eyes are like the sky.'

Amy squinted upwards. 'No, they ain't. Sky's blue, her eyes are grey.'

'But they change like the ever shifting sky.'

'Bad simile,' said Amy. 'You mean the sea.'

He waved an expansive arm. 'The sea, the sky, all of nature reminds me of Miss Vevian.'

Clarissa shuffled her feet, dropped her reticule, picked it up, dropped her fan, picked it up, and stood with her head bowed.

'It's very naughty of you to encourage such lavish compliments, Miss Vevian,' said Amy. 'Don't think Greystone would like it.'

'Miss Vevian is not Greystone's property,' said Lord Sandford haughtily.

'Not yet, she ain't,' said Amy. 'That is if you mean the engagement hasn't reached the papers.'

'Engagement?' Lord Sandford looked at Clarissa, who blushed and said, 'I should have told you. I do not know why I did not.'

Lord Sandford looked at Amy, who stood four-square in front of them and showed not the least sign of moving. Sir Jason's face rose before his eyes, painted and venomous. His head reeled. The sun was hot and he wished he had not drunk so much. He must think!

'I am sorry I arrived too late on the scene.

187

Excuse me, ladies.'

Amy watched him go. 'I'm sorry for him,' she said. 'Pleasant fellow and eminently suitable, too. But a girl like you is better off with a man taller than herself.'

'I should have said something,' said Clarissa miserably. 'But somehow I could not.'

'Never mind,' said Amy. 'Greystone's a much better catch. Oh, Lor', here come the ugly sisters.' By which she meant Bella and Angela.

'Not sisters,' said Clarissa with a grin, 'and they are both very pretty, but I know what you mean.'

Angela came fluttering up. 'What a divine hat, Miss Vevian. Oh, goldfish. Do look, Miss Vevian.'

Clarissa turned politely and looked down into the pool.

Angela put an affectionate arm about her waist and Bella stood closely on her other side.

Effy, who had been following the two ladies, moved close to Amy. 'They plan to push her in!' she said softly. 'I heard them.'

'Create a diversion! Quick!' muttered Amy. 'No, not here, silly. Over there.'

Effy tripped hurriedly away. Angela's grip on Clarissa tightened.

Often, Effy had been so worried about their circumstances that she could have screamed aloud. But it was vulgar for ladies to betray any noisy excess of emotion. Here, though, was an opportunity to let out a really good scream.

'A snake!' she cried, pointing at the grass. 'EEEEeeeeeee!'

It was a magnificent scream.

Clarissa swung round and wrenched herself free from Angela and ran towards Effy. All the guests came running as well, except Bella and Angela, who stood with their backs to the pool.

'Drat,' said Angela. 'We'll need to try again.'

'Try what?' said Amy Tribble, suddenly appearing in front of them again.

'Go away, you disgusting creature,' said Angela fiercely. 'I will never, never forgive you for what you did to me!'

'Never?' demanded Amy, her hands on her hips. 'Then I suppose it doesn't matter what I do.'

She darted forward with her hands outstretched and gave both Angela and Bella a hearty shove. Both fell backwards into the goldfish pool.

'That's what you intended to do to Miss Vevian,' said Amy.

The group around Effy had dispersed and were now running towards the goldfish pool. Amy, who had moved quickly away, could hear Angela's noisy and tearful accusations.

'Lor',' said Amy. 'Can't abide scenes.' She collected Effy and Clarissa and suggested they should leave as quickly as possible.

They had come by hired carriage and Amy had given the coachman instructions to pick them up much later. 'No matter,' she said once they were outside in the street, 'a little walk home won't harm us."

'May I offer you my escort?' said a voice behind them.

They turned round. Lord Sandford was standing there, slightly breathless, but smiling.

'That's very handsome of you,' said Amy.

'You mean I am taking my disappointment well,' he said with an infectious grin. 'But I expect to be rewarded. An offer of tea, nice strong black Bohea, to clear my brain.'

'You may have all the tea you can drink,' said Effy, fluttering her eyelashes and taking his arm and moving off with him, leaving Clarissa and Amy to follow.

'Damned ridiculous,' muttered Amy. 'Just look at her. She can't leave anything in breeches alone. But, I say, he has wonderful legs. Just look at that curve. Reminds me of a balustrade.'

Clarissa had not heard Amy in quite so relaxed or free-spoken a mood before. Amy was feeling ridiculously happy. She and Effy had another success. She had had all the fun of giving Angela and Bella a ducking. Nasty pair! She absent-mindedly began to whistle through her teeth until Clarissa pressed her hand and said, 'You whistle very well, Miss Amy, but you *are* attracting a certain amount of attention.'

'Sorry,' said Amy. 'I am so deuced happy, that's why. Another success for us, don't you see, and no violence or nasty murders either.'

'What are you talking about?' asked Clarissa. Amy told her of the happenings that had taken place at the house during the stay of their previous charge.

When she had finished, Clarissa said, 'I do not think I like adventures. I just want to settle down and have lots and lots of children.'

'That's the stuff,' said Amy. 'Here we are. I suppose we will need to invite that young man in for tea. But he deserves it. He has behaved very well, and,' she added waspishly, 'any young man who can bear the flirtings and oglings of Effy Tribble certainly deserves a reward. Before we go inside, a word in your ear, Clarissa. Next time you go anywhere socially, you must say to yourself, "I am going to marry the Earl of Greystone – the *handsome* Earl of Greystone. I. Clarissa Vevian. And not some chattering little miss with more hair than wit like Chloris Deveney." That should give you bags of confidence.'

Effy had entered the hall ahead of them, with Lord Sandford behind her. As Amy and Clarissa entered, they heard Effy say, 'Oh, Harris, do not keep on plaguing me about the disappearance of Mrs Loomis. Have tea brought up to the drawing room, right away.'

Lord Sandford stood aside to let the ladies go first, his mind still racing. He had been a fool to waste his time on Clarissa Vevian. He should have courted old Effy Tribble instead!

He felt better after the walk. His head had begun to clear. He gratefully drank two cups of strong tea and wondered how to get Clarissa alone to see if he could get the papers.

He decided to see if he could get upstairs to the bedrooms unnoticed. He rose to his feet. 'May I be excused, ladies?

Since he did not pick up his hat and gloves, no one was rude enough to ask him where he was going. His destination was obvious.

Once outside the drawing room, he took a deep breath and darted for the stairs. He let out a yelp of surprise as he nearly bumped into a small housemaid.

'I beg your pardon,' he said. 'I was looking for the ... er.'

'The Jericho, my lord. It's in the garding. This way, my lord.'

Cursing under his breath, he followed her downstairs, where he was turned over to a tall footman who then conducted him out to the earth closet in the garden and then conducted him all the way back up the stairs to the drawing room.

'More tea?' Amy asked.

He did not want any more tea but he simply had to stay as long as possible. Had Greystone not spiked his guns, he would have asked leave to pay his addresses to Miss Vevian and then begged a few moments in private with her.

'Yes,' he said. 'I am still very thirsty.'

He was just holding out his cup when Harris entered. He addressed the Tribbles. 'There is a person from the constabulary to see you,' he said. He added with gloomy relish, 'Mrs Loomis, the housekeeper, has been found.'

'Then where is she?' demanded Amy as she and Effy got to their feet.

'Dead as a doornail, with a knife stuck in her heart.'

Effy turned pale and Amy put an arm about her and snapped at the butler, 'Stop enjoying yourself, you ghoul, and conduct us downstairs.'

'I was merely giving you the facts,' said Harris, sounding injured. 'The constable found this address in the pocket of her petticoat when they was searching the body. He wishes you to view the corpse and identify it proper.'

'I don't think I can,' said Effy.

'Oh, I'll do it,' said Amy, 'but come along with me, Effy. Sandford, you must see yourself out. No, Clarissa, we don't need you. Practise your scales or read some Italian or something.'

'How dreadful,' said Clarissa when they had gone.

'Shocking things happen in London,' said Lord Sandford mournfully. 'I am glad to have this opportunity to speak to you alone, Miss Vevian.'

'Oh, no, please don't,' begged Clarissa. 'I should be most embarrassed. I humbly apologize for having obviously given you the wrong idea.'

'No, no, nothing to do with that,' he said hurriedly. He stopped and listened. Voices from the hall and then the slamming of the street door. The Tribbles had gone.

'I have a confession to make, Miss Vevian,' he began, twinkling at her in a boyish manner. 'A few years ago I became embroiled in a liaison with a married lady. She wrote very passionate letters to me. I should not have kept them. My valet stole various items from me, along with the packet of letters. He was staying at The Bell at the same time as yourself and hid the letters in the bottom of your jewel box. You see, evidently the militia arrived to look for some government papers and he hid the stolen items in various rooms. All were recovered, but I could not ask too closely about the letters. The poor fellow repented of the theft and confided everything to me. Should the letters fall into the wrong hands, the poor lady might be blackmailed.'

Clarissa remembered that rabbity young man. But he hadn't looked like a valet. She was still shocked at the news of the murder of the housekeeper and could not think clearly. She moved her hands in a helpless way and said, 'But there is nothing but jewellery in my jewel box.'

'Oh, please go and look again,' he said. 'I beg you.'

'Very well,' said Clarissa. 'Wait here.'

On her way up to her bedroom, she met Baxter, the Tribbles' lady's maid, who was dressed to go out. 'They should have taken me with them,' said Baxter. 'Miss Effy's bound to have hysterics. If you are looking for Hubbard, miss, she has the headache and is lying down in her room. I am just going to join my two ladies.'

'Do what you can to help them,' said Clarissa. 'Poor Mrs Loomis.'

'It's a wicked city, this,' said Baxter.

She went on down the stairs. Clarissa went up to her room and threw back the lid of her jewel box and lifted out the trays. She moved aside necklaces and bracelets and felt at the bottom of the box. Her fingers touched what she had previously assumed to be packing which Hubbard had put at the bottom. Her eyes widened. She searched for the corners until she found an edge and pulled out a flat packet sealed in black oilskin.

And then her heart began to hammer against her ribs. What if this contained the missing government papers? She could not hand the packet to Lord Sandford without making sure. The packet was stitched all round. She found her sewing scissors and loosened the stitches along one edge and drew the papers out. One brief look was enough. Clarissa turned white. Her first impulse was to call for help. But just as she opened her mouth to shout, she closed it again. Whom could she trust? Only Hubbard, who would scream the place down. Someone had been in her room that night. Any of the servants might be aiding and abetting the spies.

She must get rid of Sandford and then wait for Amy and Effy to return. She seized a novel and quickly cut out several of the pages and then, forcing herself to be calm, she put them in the packet instead of the government papers and stitched up the packet again.

She shoved the government papers under her mattress, picked up the packet, and ran down the stairs.

'What an age you have been!' cried Lord Sandford. He saw the packet in Clarissa's hands and darted forward and seized it. 'Thank you. I shall be ever grateful to you, Miss Vevian.'

Clarissa looked at him solemnly. 'You had better be on your way, my lord,' she said. 'You should not be alone with me when my chaperones are absent.'

'Servant, ma'am,' he cried, seizing her hand and kissing it. He ran from the room. Clarissa crossed to the window, opened it and leaned out. He emerged after only a few moments and ran off down the street.

She sat down with her legs trembling. Should she put on her bonnet and go to the nearest magistrate? But look what had happened to Mrs Loomis. That could have just been a straightforward murder not connected with any spies, but Clarissa was sure it was not. Amy and Effy could not be long. All she had to do was sit tight and wait.

Lord Sandford ran all the way to his club, sure of finding Sir Jason there. Sir Jason was lounging in the coffee room, reading a newspaper.

'Got 'em,' said Lord Sandford triumphantly.

Sir Jason smiled. 'You see how easy it is to clear your debts? That packet is worth a fortune to us. Now we walk to a certain address where arrangements will be made for your trip to Paris.'

They strolled together in the direction of

Charing Cross. The fine weather was beginning to break. The sky was becoming dark.

At last they arrived at a seedy tenement in a long street which led down to Hungerford Stairs. Sir Jason led the way up to the first landing and rapped twice on the door. 'Enter,' called a voice.

They went into a darkened room furnished only with a table and three chairs. A small sallow man was sitting at the table. 'Mr Ryan, who will arrange your journey and supply you with enough money to live in Paris like a king,' said Sir Jason expansively.

'The papers,' demanded Mr Ryan in a hoarse voice. Sir Jason threw the packet down on the desk.

'Good,' said Mr Ryan, fingering the packet. Then his eyes narrowed. 'What is this?' he demanded.

'What is what, dear fellow?' asked Sir Jason.

'The stitching down this side is new and of white thread. I assume you checked the papers and sewed the packet up again yourself.'

There was a long silence. Sir Jason turned and looked at Lord Sandford, his eyes flat and obsidian.

'No, I didn't look,' said Lord Sandford. 'Bound to be right, though. She didn't suspect a thing.'

Mr Ryan took out a long slim knife and sliced the white stitching. He drew out the papers and looked down at them. Then he raised his eyes and looked at Lord Sandford.

'These are pages cut out of a novel,' he said.

Sir Jason moved like lightning. He struck Lord Sandford full across the face, his diamond ring gashing the young man's cheek.

'Damn you!' shouted Lord Sandford, raising his fists.

Then he lowered them. Mr Ryan had drawn out a pistol and was levelling it at him.

Sir Jason looked at Lord Sandford with contempt. 'Has she had time to go to the authorities?'

'Perhaps not,' said Lord Sandford. 'She was alone, apart from the servants. Those Tribbles had to go off to identify some body. Their housekeeper has been found murdered.'

'Then all may not yet be lost,' said Sir Jason. He looked at Ryan. 'I will need to leave the country. I will be back here shortly.' He moved to the door.

'What about me?' cried Lord Sandford.

Sir Jason did not look at him. He looked at

Mr Ryan instead.

'Get rid of this fool,' he said, and then he went out and shut the door behind him.

Clarissa paced nervously up and down the drawing room. Night was falling and the Tribbles had still not returned. There was nothing for it. She would need to get the papers and go out and get help.

Harris entered with a card on a tray. 'Sir Jason Pym has called, miss.'

'Enter first murderer,' thought Clarissa wildly, remembering the story of the widow of Brighton. 'Tell Sir Jason we are not at home,' she said firmly. When Harris had left, she sat down suddenly. Her knees were shaking.

She would wait until he left, give him good time to get away, and then she would make her escape. If only there were someone she could trust. There was Yvette, but Yvette was so heavy with child she could barely move, and it would take ages to get some sense into Hubbard's head. She thought of the household servants, but her frantic mind began to imbue them all with sinister features.

She heard Harris mounting the stairs again and called, 'Has he gone?'

'Yes, miss,' called Harris.

'Then where are you going?'

'I am calling all the staff down to the servants' hall, miss. There has been a theft from the kitchen.'

'A theft of what?' called Clarissa with a hysterical edge to her voice. There was a silence, and then Harris's voice came again. 'A skillet, miss.'

Clarissa waited. With all the servants in the hall down in the basement, she would be able to slip out of the house unnoticed. She would wait until she heard them descend, wait a little longer, and then go up to her room and get those papers.

She felt very young and weak and helpless. She wanted her mother. She wanted the Earl of Greystone. She wanted the Tribbles.

Harris could not get Yvette to move. She was lying on her bed, her face covered with a thin film of sweat. 'I think my time has come,' she said.

The butler decided to leave her. There was only Hubbard to rouse and push, protesting, down the stairs.

Grumbling, Hubbard went into the servants' hall and then let out a scream. Sir Jason was standing at one end with a pistol levelled at the servants, who were huddled at the other. 'Good,' said Sir Jason. 'Lock

202

the area door and give me the key.'

Whimpering with fright, Hubbard went to join the other servants.

When Harris handed him the key, Sir Jason put it in his pocket and then backed away to the door of the servants' hall. 'Remember, all of you,' he said. 'One cry for help, one attempt to escape, and I will kill Miss Vevian first and then all of you.'

He went out of the servants' hall and locked them in, and then ran up the stairs.

'What do you want?' demanded Clarissa, and then she saw the pistol in his hand.

'The papers,' he said. 'Get them.'

And then down below the street door slammed. The Tribbles had come home.

He pressed the pistol into Clarissa's side. 'Call them,' he said.

Clarissa called through white lips, 'Miss Amy! Miss Effy.'

She heard Amy's answering call and then footsteps on the stairs.

'Do not harm them,' she whispered. 'I will give you the papers.'

Amy, Effy, and Baxter came into the drawing room. They saw Sir Jason holding the pistol against Clarissa's side. 'Over by the window, all of you,' he said. He pushed Clarissa a little way and stood with the pistol covering them all.

Then from the top of the house came a long, loud scream.

'Yvette!' said Amy, identifying that scream. 'She has gone into labour. I don't know what you want, but in God's mercy, sir, I beg you to let me go to her.'

'Shut up!' said Sir Jason. 'You stay here while Miss Vevian gets me some papers from her room. If you move from here or call for help, I will kill her.'

Yvette screamed again.

'And I'll silence that noisy wench when I'm up there,' he snarled.

Amy had never thought so frantically or so quickly in all her life. She wanted that baby of Yvette's. The house in Holles Street should have that baby. She and Effy were past the age of child-bearing, and all Amy's frustrated maternal feelings had concentrated on that baby.

'Wait!' she said. 'She does not have the papers. I have.'

She looked at Clarissa as she spoke, her whole mind screaming a silent message to the girl to be quiet.

'They're here,' she said, kneeling down by a low cupboard in the corner.

Effy knew what Amy was going to do and

let out a bleat of fright and clutched hold of Baxter. There were no papers in that cupboard but there was a hideous stuffed cobra which Mr Haddon had brought back from India and given to Amy as a present.

'Here they are!' said Amy. She seized the cobra and flung it full at Sir Jason.

What he saw flying towards him was a hideous venomous snake with glaring eyes. He threw up his hands to protect his face, and Miss Amy Tribble flew clean across the room and brought him down by cannoning into him with all her force.

Winded and desperate, he squirmed on the floor, his hands reaching for the pistol he had dropped.

Clarissa jumped down on his searching hand with all her force while Effy seized the pistol and held it in one shaking hand.

'Don't just stand there!' howled Amy, sitting up. 'Hit him with something!'

Sir Jason struggled to his feet and made a dive for the door. Effy closed her eyes tightly and pulled the trigger and then howled with pain as the recoil from the pistol sprained her wrist.

Sir Jason fell face-down on the floor, a dark-red stain spreading through the back of his coat.

'A flush hit,' cried Amy.

Effy swayed and dropped the pistol.

'No, you don't,' said Amy. 'No time for fainting. Yvette needs us. Come along. Clarissa, go and see what has happened to the servants.'

'But him?' whispered Clarissa.

'He's dead, ain't he?' snapped Amy. 'Harris can go for the constable.'

Clarissa ran down the stairs and then stood swaying in the hall, overcome with dizziness. There came a thundering knock at the door. 'Greystone! Open up!' called the earl's voice.

Clarissa wrenched open the door and tumbled into his arms, crying incoherently about papers, and snakes, and Yvette's baby.

'Where are the servants?' he asked.

'I think he must have locked them in.'

'Who?'

'Sir Jason Pym.'

'And where is he now?'

'Dead. Upstairs. Miss Effy shot him.'

He pushed her into a chair in the hall and told her firmly not to move. He unlocked the door of the servants' hall and cut through the babble of exclamations by telling Hubbard first to attend to her mistress, the footmen and the knife-boy to run for help, and the maids to make themselves useful.

He then raced upstairs to the drawing room and recoiled in horror at the sight that met his eyes. Sir Jason was lying face down on the floor with a hideous snake reared above him. It took him a few moments to realize the snake was stuffed.

He then went farther up to where the screams were coming from.

'No place for a gentleman,' said Amy, barring his way. 'Yvette is having her baby. Go to Clarissa.'

It was to be a long night. At first, it was only the parish constable, then the magistrate, then the militia, and then a deputation of gentlemen from the War Office. Clarissa told her story over and over again while the earl held tightly on to her hand.

'We'll get Sandford,' said the earl at last. 'But we don't know who the rest are.'

Mr Haddon and Mr Randolph had arrived to swell the throng, followed by Angela and Bella, who had called to complain about Amy and found no one wanted to hear so trivial a story.

Clarissa had handed over the papers. Numb with horror, she heard of the death of Epsom and how it was more than likely that Sir Jason had killed Mrs Loomis too.

The gentlemen from the War Office were rising to take their leave when the two Tribble sisters appeared in the drawing room. They were hot and dishevelled. Effy was crying quietly.

'It's a boy!' said Amy. 'Oh, Lord save us all, we've got a boy!'

When Sir Jason had left, Lord Sandford backed away from Mr Ryan. 'Look, old chap,' he said, trying to smile, 'what say I go away and forget about the whole thing?'

Mr Ryan smiled and raised the pistol.

Lord Sandford looked at him in horror. 'You are going to kill me. Why?'

'Because your very incompetence is a danger to us,' said Mr Ryan calmly.

Lord Sandford went very still. Inside he felt cold yet suddenly calm and calculating. He affected to tremble and his hands scrabbled on the table top as he cried, 'Oh, spare me! I will get my father to pay you anything you ask. Spare me!'

Mr Ryan looked at him, the contempt in his eyes mixed with cupidity. Perhaps he could fleece this young buck before disposing of him. He lowered the pistol slightly. Lord Sandford's groping fingers closed over a paperknife on the table.

'Yes, yes,' babbled Lord Sandlord. 'You must not kill me. You must listen to me!'

'Perhaps we might do business,' said Mr Ryan, leaning forward and placing the hand which still held the pistol on the table.

Lord Sandford struck like a snake. He drove the paperknife into Mr Ryan's neck with the force of a madman.

Mr Ryan fell forward, blood gushing from the wound in his neck, his eyes already glazing over as the life poured out of him.

Lord Sandford got slowly to his feet. Soon the whole country would be looking for him, of that he was certain.

Miss Vevian knew about the papers and would surely not be sitting waiting for Sir Jason to arrive.

He would need to get out of the country. There were two drawers in the table. He pushed Mr Ryan's body onto the floor and slid them open. In one, he found a great pile of banknotes and a bag of guineas. He stuffed the money into his pockets. In the other drawer was a small notebook with a list of names. He balanced it in his hand. How many of the names listed were young fellows like himself who had been lured into treason by Sir Jason?

Damn Sir Jason. Lord Sandford thirsted for

revenge. He put the notebook in his pocket. He left the room and made his way through the streets until he found a second-hand clothes shop. He bought himself a plain drab suit. Then he went to a wig maker's and bought a large full-bottomed wig. He could not risk hiring a room at an inn to effect the change. He forced himself to return to Ryan's.

Soon, he had effected the transformation.

He went out to Charing Cross and hired a hack. He asked to be taken to the main post office in the city. Once there, he asked for pen and ink and sat down and wrote a long letter of explanation and apology to a general at the War Office whose name he had read recently in the newspapers. He then enclosed the notebook he had taken from Ryan and sealed them together in a packet and sent them off.

Feeling much better, he hired a horse from a livery stable and rode out of London, keeping away from the main roads. This way, it would take him a long time to reach the coast. But he was alive and free. He began to whistle.

8

Comrades, you may pass the rosy. With
  permission of the chair,
I shall leave you for a little, for I'd like to take
  the air.
Whether 'twas the sauce at dinner, or that glass
  of ginger beer,
Or these strong cheroots, I know not, but I feel a
  little queer.
Sir Theodore Martin

The Tribbles were a sensation. Effy Tribble
had shot down a dangerous spy, aided by
her sister, Amy – which was rather hard on
Amy, who had been the real heroine of the
piece.

At first, they both enjoyed the notoriety
immensely. The tale of the spies was talked
about over and over again as their drawing
room was filled day after day by an eager
audience. The notebook which Lord Sandford had sent to the War Office meant many
arrests and more sensation.

And then as the weeks passed, Amy and

Effy began to settle down again and feel very tired indeed. Yvette was a good mother, but nothing stopped either of the Tribbles from waking at the slightest cry from that precious baby. He was to be called George after the king, despite Yvette's unpatriotic protests that she did not want her son to be named after a madman. Amy pointed out that the Prince Regent was also called George, which did not please Yvette either. She said the prince was a lecher and a drunk. But she was so grateful to the Tribbles that she at last agreed, and so George it was – a small black-haired baby who ruled the house in Holles Street.

To Clarissa's amusement, Mr Haddon and Mr Randolph, the nabobs, were every bit as doting as the Tribbles and sat in the evenings planning out the education of the boy.

She was to leave soon and go back home to Bath, where her delighted parents were preparing for her wedding. Lord Greystone was to escort her. Much as she loved the Tribbles, she longed for her day of departure, for the Tribbles had become very strict chaperones indeed and did not seem to trust the earl alone with Clarissa.

Clarissa was rarely clumsy these days. She did break a cream jug and fall over a table, but these incidents were considered minor in one who had once been capable of setting carpets on fire.

The one thing that dimmed Clarissa's happiness was the prospect of living with Angela and Bella. They would all be together in the earl's home near Marlborough, and at times she felt she could not bear the idea.

She held her dislike in check but it was always there, polluting the atmosphere.

One day, when she was sitting alone in the drawing room, the earl came in. He looked about and raised his eyebrows in surprise. 'I never thought to see you alone again, my sweeting,' he said. 'Come and kiss me. I have great news.'

'What is it?' asked Clarissa.

'Kiss first. News afterwards.'

She melted into his arms. 'Oh, that is so very good,' he sighed at last. 'Kiss me again.'

They sank down together on the sofa, kissing wildly. He was just bending her backwards, his lips seeking her neck, when a peremptory cough startled them both. Clarissa sat up, blushing and straightening her hair.

'Lord Greystone!' said Effy Tribble severely. 'You should know better. Not until after you are married.'

'How very strict you are,' he said. Amy

came into the room.

'He's been at it again,' said Effy primly.

'At what? asked Amy with interest.

'*You* know. Kissing and cuddling.'

'Oh, dear. Do try to restrain yourself, my lord,' said Amy, making the earl feel sixteen years old.

'What is your news, Greystone?' asked Clarissa hurriedly.

'Wonderful news for us. Bella is engaged to be married, to Baron Smithfield, the very *rich* Baron Smithfield. Angela says she will live with Bella after they are married.'

'And what of the boys?' asked Clarissa anxiously.

'They too.'

'What a relief,' exclaimed Clarissa. 'Does that mean we can both lead a nice dull quiet life?'

'As dull and quiet as you like. The Misses Tribble will no doubt go on being a sensation.'

'I hope not,' said Amy anxiously. 'We need another client and I really don't know how we are going to get one. Now Mrs Edgefield, that rich widow who lives in Park Lane, her daughter is spoilt to a fault and as ugly as a boot besides. I said to her, I said, "Why do you not turn your Helen over to us? Look what successes we have had." And she said, very stiffly on her stiffs, "Could not contemplate sending my ewe lamb into a household where everyone gets murdered." "Would you rather have her a spinster?" says I, for Helen is as ugly as a toad. But I had forgot how blind mothers can be. "There is no question of that," says she. "No girl with my Helen's looks and dowry need ever want for a husband." Such a fool. You should see Helen Edgefield. Any man getting his leg over that would need to put a bag over her head first.'

'The reason we cannot get anyone,' said Effy icily, 'is because of your shocking vulgarity, Amy. Have you ever heard a coarse expression pass my lips? I do not know how poor Mr Haddon and Mr Randolph can bear your company of an evening without shuddering.'

'Ho! Look at who is talking. Do you never think, dear sis, that mothers might shy away from this house because you look like a demirep with those eyelashes of yours painted black and your shrivelled body showing itself through near-transparent muslin?'

'You are jealous,' screeched Effy. 'No man is ever going to look at you unless he has a penchant for broken-down cab-horses!'

'Ladies! Ladies!' begged Clarissa.

'I do all the work while you swan around,' said Amy passionately. 'We need money to care for little George, to give him a decent home, but all you do is sit on your bum and sigh and hope by some miracle the work will come to you.'

'That is not true. Why, only the other day I asked Lady Strutton if we could not sponsor her Charlotte. And she said it was out of the question as her Charlotte was very delicate and *refined* and she said that Amy Tribble's coarseness would send her into a spasm.'

'Oh!' said Amy weakly, all the fight going out of her.

'Now, Miss Effy,' chided Clarissa, 'I do not believe a word of that. You just made it up to score a point.'

'Did you?' demanded Amy.

'Well ... yes,' said Effy, 'but I am sure that was what she meant.'

Amy, tired of quarrelling, sat down. 'I think Clarissa is our last client and we'd best face up to it and think of something else.'

'Oh, no,' said Clarissa. 'You must let me be your advertisement. You must let me tell all the Bath ladies of your successes. You will have someone else soon. You'll see.'

The day of Clarissa's departure soon arrived. She felt a lump rising in her throat as she hugged Effy and Amy and told them they were expected to arrive in time for the wedding. 'And I am sure I shall be able to find a client for you by then,' she said.

Yvette, looking very French and matronly, stood holding baby George. Clarissa kissed the baby and gave Yvette a purse of gold. Then she walked out to the carriage where the earl was waiting. Amy and Effy went with her.

'Do you not think,' said Clarissa, her foot on the step, 'that you might not use your great talents to find a husband for Yvette?'

Amy and Effy looked startled. 'Then, you see, there could be a proper christening,' went on Clarissa. 'She is a handsome lady and still young. I am sure some man would be glad to wed her in return for a certain security.'

Amy looked at the ground. 'But a man would take her – and George – away from us.'

'But it would be better for little George in the long run,' said Clarissa.

'We love her and George,' said Effy, 'which is more than some fellow who merely married her for money would do.'

'Then make sure she meets suitable men and then someone might fall in love with her.'

'We'll try,' said Amy reluctantly.

Clarissa hugged them again and climbed into the carriage. She pulled down the window and leaned out. 'Thank you for everything,' she said, gratitude making her eyes fill with tears so that the two sisters were a blurred image. The carriage began to move. 'Thank you for saving my life,' called Clarissa. The carriage reached the corner of the street. 'I love you!' called Clarissa, and then subsided back in her seat, took out her handkerchief and dabbed her eyes.

'I shall become jealous of the Tribbles if you go on like that,' said the earl, putting an arm around her.

A cough like a dog's bark came from Hubbard, sitting opposite. The earl sighed and removed his arm. Like Clarissa, he had forgotten they would be chaperoned by Hubbard on the road to Bath. They were to be married in a month's time, but right at that moment, it seemed like a lifetime away to the Earl of Greystone.

'Well, that's that,' said Amy, drying her eyes. 'I wish God would send us another like

Clarissa Vevian.'

'A splendid girl,' said Effy, 'but I hope the next one will be someone a leetle smaller.'

'If there is a next one,' said Amy gloomily.

Clarissa's fame had spread to Bath. Everyone wanted to know all about her adventures and she became weary of telling the same story over and over again. Each time, she praised the Tribble sisters to the skies, but the disappointing response was usually that Clarissa was terribly brave but their little Mary, or Beth or Dorothy, would simply have died of fright in such a household. Clarissa began to despair of ever finding anyone for the Tribbles.

But her praises of them had not fallen on totally deaf ears. Clarissa was walking in the pump room with her mother when a certain Mrs Kendall approached them, smiling broadly.

'Mushroom,' whispered the Lady Clarendon, giving Clarissa's arm a pinch. 'Cut her!'

But soft-hearted Clarissa found it impossible to cut anyone who looked so genial, and to her mother's fury she stopped and gave the lady a brief curtsy.

'I am Mrs Kendall, Lady Clarendon, Miss Vevian,' said the stout woman. Lady Clarendon stared straight ahead. Clarissa smiled encouragingly.

'The truth is,' said Mrs Kendall, 'I'm that worried about my Maria. I'm not a one for pushing my way in and I never speak to my betters without an introduction...'

'Quite right too,' said Lady Clarendon firmly.

'But,' went on Mrs Kendall, pretending not to hear, 'when I heard you was brought out in London by them Tribbles and how good they were, I wondered if they might do anything with my Maria. My husband says to me, he says, you don't want to send her off to that household where they have more murders than we have had hot dinners, but things is desperate, that's what I said.'

'They are coming here to my wedding,' said Clarissa, ignoring her mother's glare, 'and, if you would like it, they could call on you before they leave Bath.'

'That would be fine,' said Mrs Kendall. She took out a card. 'That's my address. Are they very dear?'

'Very,' said Clarissa coolly, 'but worth every penny. If you cannot afford much, I would not trouble them.'

'Money's no problem,' said Mrs Kendall. 'Why, Mr Kendall could buy up the most of

Bath if he wanted. Thank you, my lady, Miss Vevian, thanks ever so.'

'Did those Tribbles not train you how to depress the attentions of the vulgar?' demanded Lady Clarendon as she and Clarissa walked on.

'They taught me to be kind and polite to all,' said Clarissa. 'I do wish Greystone would come to Bath earlier, but he is preparing things for us at his home.'

'Well, I must confess the Tribbles did sterling work with you, Clarissa,' said Lady Clarendon in a mollified voice. 'I do not suppose, however, as they are spinsters, that they had an opportunity to talk to you about the ... er ... more delicate side of marriage.'

'No, Mama.'

Lady Clarendon sighed. 'I suppose I had better warn you...'

'Warn me about what, Mama?' demanded Clarissa sharply.

'Not here. Let us take a stroll in the Parade Gardens.'

Clarissa waited impatiently until the viscountess obviously considered no one could overhear what she was about to say. She sat down on a bench and drew Clarissa down beside her.

'Do you know, Clarissa, what a man does

to a woman in the marriage bed?'

Clarissa was dreadfully embarrassed. 'He hugs and kisses – I mean, the husband.'

'There is more to it than hugs and kisses. You will lose your virginity and must be prepared for the pain and suffering of that.'

'Pain and suffering?' repeated Clarissa, aghast.

'After the initial experience, it becomes easier. But you will have demands made on your body which will seem *very* odd and shocking to you. Remember at all times, it is your duty to obey your husband. Some nights, it might seem nigh unbearable and you will wish you could simply go to bed and sleep, but take a stiff drink of brandy and lie back and think of something else until it is all over.'

'But what of love and romance? Do they not exist? What am I saying? I *know* they exist!'

Lady Clarendon patted her daughter's hand. 'They are part of courtship, not marriage. Enjoy yourself while you may.'

And glad to have done her duty, she rose to her feet to indicate the lecture was over. Clarissa fell up the steps leaving the garden. She opened her parasol with such force that the spokes went clean through the silk, then threw the ruined parasol away without looking so that it struck a flower seller in the face and the irritated Lady Clarendon had to buy great armfuls of flowers to calm the outraged vendor.

Mrs Kendall, her husband and daughter lived in a house in Milsom Street. Mr Kendall had made a great deal of money out of coal-mines in the north, sold out and moved to Bath. Their daughter, Maria, had been born when they were both forty. Maria was the reason for the move to Bath. Both Mr and Mrs Kendall were small, fat, and plain. As Maria grew, so she increased in beauty, and the more beautiful she became, the more rampant grew the Kendalls' social ambitions. With Maria's looks and her father's money, surely she could secure a lord at the very least!

But as Maria reached her nineteenth year, her doting parents found that she was ... not there. She lived in a dream world that seemed to run like a perpetual play in her head, with ogres and villains, heroes and heroines. She lived inside her private world and paid no heed to the line of suitors attracted by her father's wealth and her great beauty.

Maria Kendall *was* beautiful. She was small

and dainty with a small head, luxuriant chestnut-brown hair, large green eyes, a small pink mouth, and a straight nose. Her movements were graceful, and just occasionally, when she was paying attention to someone or something, she showed great charm.

To Mr and Mrs Kendall, with their gross appetites and their love of showy finery, dreamy Maria was a great disappointment. Despite her vagueness and dreaminess, she did show a stubborn streak when asked, pleaded, *begged* to accept some gentleman's hand in marriage. The Kendalls had thought up various punishments to try to bring her to a sense of her own folly, but nothing seemed to work. Long sessions of incarceration in her room and a diet of bread and water did nothing else but make her thin and pale and alarm them into releasing her and putting her back on proper meals. The birch rod only marked her fair skin. The burning of all her favourite books caused tears but no improvement in her manner.

'I am at my wit's end, Mr Kendall,' said Mrs Kendall, returning from the pump room after speaking to Clarissa. 'So you know what I did?'

'No, my love,' said Mr Kendall, easing his

gouty foot.

'I went up to that there Miss Clarissa Vevian, her what was brought out by those Tribble sisters in London and got herself the Earl of Greystone, and I asked her about them Tribbles. A very nice young lady she is, too, not like that cold pudding-faced mother of hers. She told me the Tribbles was coming to her wedding and she would tell them about our Maria and send them round. There!'

Mr Kendall straightened up. 'You mean – send her away to strangers?. In London? Here, them Tribbles was in all the news-papers. Killed a man, they did. Not ladylike.'

'Do we care?' snorted Mrs Kendall. 'This Clarissa Vevian is a great giant of a girl with red hair. *Red* hair, mark you, and yet she's to be the Countess of Greystone. If they can get an earl for her, think what they could get for Maria.'

'They could get the Prince Regent for Maria and Maria would say no,' said Mr Kendall cynically.

'And quite right, too,' retorted Mrs Kendall. 'Him a married man and all. We've tried everything. Them Tribbles are our last hope.'

'What if they don't take her?'

'Course they'll take her. They're doing it for money.'

'Well,' said Mr Kendall. He broke off as Maria came into the room. She looked a picture in pink-sprigged muslin. She gave them a sweet unfocused smile, picked up a book from the sofa, and walked out again.

'You're right,' said Mr Kendall heavily. 'We'll pay them Tribble women what they want, just so long as they guarantee to get her a husband!'

Amy and Effy, escorted by Mr Haddon and Mr Randolph, arrived in Bath. Amy and Effy were prepared to accept modestly all the compliments that would surely be showered on them by Clarissa's grateful parents. But although their reception was warm, although they were formally thanked and given a generous present of money as a bonus from the viscount, they could not help noticing a certain frost in the air.

Clarissa was delighted to see them, but she looked wan and pale and had shadows under her eyes. They soon found out the reason why her parents were not so enthusiastic as they might have been.

Poor Clarissa was clumsy once more. She slouched, she dropped things, she made sudden ungainly movements and swiped ornaments from tables and shelves.

After a week of seeing Clarissa becoming more awkward and wretched, the sisters, Mr Haddon, and Mr Randolph met in the coffee room of the hotel in which the gentlemen had been billeted – the sisters themselves staying with Clarissa and her parents – to discuss the problem.

'I don't like Lady Clarendon, and that's a fact,' said Amy crossly. 'Clarissa adores her mother, but Lady Clarendon does nothing but complain about the girl and criticize her.'

'Perhaps she has had a row with Greystone,' suggested Mr Haddon. 'I mean, I am sure if he still loved her and she knew it, then she would not be so sad and worried.'

Effy shook her head. 'I took it upon myself to question Clarissa's maid, Hubbard. Hubbard said that Greystone took a most affectionate leave of her.'

'Why can't he come to Bath?' asked Amy. 'He is due to arrive on the day of the wedding rehearsal, but we need him here now.'

'Have you asked Miss Vevian herself what is wrong?' demanded Mr Randolph, adjusting the lace at his cuffs. Like Mr Haddon, Mr Randolph had firmly attached himself to the Tribble sisters and considered himself 'one of the family'. He would have been dismayed and startled had he known that both sisters viewed him in the light of a prospective husband. He enjoyed their admiration of his fine clothes and their warm appreciation of his lavish presents, but although the sisters were the same age as he, he was not worldly-wise enough to know that a lady's romantic heart never grows old.

'I asked her,' said Amy. 'She said the most odd thing. She said, "Have you ever been married, Miss Amy?" When I said no, she said that in that case I could not help. I was about to press further when her mother came into the room and started fussing about, you know the way she does. "Sit up straight, Clarissa. Don't slouch. Really, Miss Tribble, I had begun to hope you had cured her of her clumsiness."

There was a long silence.

Then Mr Haddon said suddenly, 'Bride nerves.'

'Eh?' demanded Amy.

He coughed delicately. 'Bride nerves. It is quite common, you know.'

'But if she loves him and he loves her, what has she got to be nervous about? said Effy. 'I would have thought she would have been in high alt at the prospect of soon being with her husband and mistress of her own household. What can you mean, Mr Haddon?'

'How shall I put it?' Mr Haddon looked at the smoke-blackened beams of the ceiling as if seeking inspiration in them. 'The prospect of the physical side of marriage is sometimes frightening to a young girl.'

All immediately could not help thinking of what the physical side of marriage entailed and the Tribble sisters shared a communal blush.

'Surely her mother has spoken to her about that,' suggested Mr Randolph.

There was another meditative silence and then Amy said slowly, 'Do you know, the countess probably *has* spoken to her and terrified her out of her wits. I'll talk to her myself.'

Three pairs of eyes looked at Amy Tribble. Three racing minds wondered what Miss Amy knew about the subject, but Effy dared not mention anything for fear of Amy's delivering herself of some terribly crude remark.

It was finally agreed that Amy should try to talk to Clarissa further, but Amy soon found that this was a hard thing to do. Clarissa was receiving the last fittings for her wedding gown and trousseau. Relatives were arriving in droves. There was no space left in the house and so Hubbard, who had had to surrender her room to house three visiting servants, slept on a bed placed in Clarissa's room and was always present.

When the Earl of Greystone arrived on the day of the wedding rehearsal, things were no better. The rehearsal was a disaster. Clarissa literally tripped up the aisle and nearly cannoned into the earl.

'For goodness' sake!' shouted her mother, 'cannot you contrive to behave yourself like a lady for this one all-important occasion?'

When they filed out of the church after that disastrous rehearsal, Amy felt like killing first the viscountess and then the viscount, and then all the sniggering relatives.

Summoning up her courage, Amy drew the earl aside. 'I must talk to you in private,' she said. 'It is about Clarissa.'

He nodded. 'Get into my carriage, Miss Amy, and I will drive you back.'

Amy waited impatiently until he climbed in and took the reins:

'Now,' he said as his horses clopped through the sedate streets of Bath and then began the long climb up the Royal Crescent, 'what is the matter?'

'This is awfully difficult,' said Amy miserably. 'You may have remarked, my lord, that Clarissa is not herself. I have noticed she is only clumsy when she is unhappy and she is very unhappy.'

'Her mother is enough to make any girl unhappy,' he said. 'She is a silly thoughtless woman who has never quite forgiven Clarissa for not turning out a pattern of herself.'

'I think she may have had a talk with Clarissa about ... er, hum ... what to expect on her wedding night,' said Amy.

He looked at Amy's embarrassed face with affection. 'Your concern does you credit, Miss Amy, but my Clarissa is not a simpering Bath miss.'

'Your Clarissa is a young Bath virgin,' said Amy roundly. 'Please, my lord, could you meet her tonight after they have all gone to bed? I beg of you to ask her what is wrong or she will contrive to break her neck or someone else's at the wedding tomorrow out of sheer nerves.'

He sighed. 'It does seem an age since I have seen her alone. Everyone will retire early tonight. Where should I meet her?'

'Away from the house,' said Amy urgently. 'Outside. You could meet outside on the pavement and take a little walk and talk about things. Her maid sleeps in her room but I think I know how to put her out of action.'

'Do that for me,' he said. 'I shall be waiting at midnight.'

After dinner, Amy summoned Hubbard to her room. 'You are a good and loyal servant, Hubbard,' said Amy, 'and I called you here so that we could both drink a toast to the happy couple.'

Hubbard was most gratified. Amy Tribble might be odd, but she was good *ton* and here she was, prepared to chat and drink on equal terms with a lady's maid.

Later that evening, Clarissa looked up in surprise as Amy Tribble entered, half dragging Hubbard.

'Help me get her to bed,' urged Amy. 'Yes, I know she's drunk. Don't ask questions. Do as you are told. You are to meet Greystone outside in the street at midnight. Do not let anyone see you leaving.'

'But why?' asked Clarissa, struggling to help Hubbard out of her clothes.

'Just do as I say,' said Amy fiercely.

At midnight, Clarissa wrapped herself in a long cloak and slipped quietly from the house. She hesitated outside the house and then saw a tall figure striding towards her.

'Good evening, Greystone,' she whispered.

'Clarissa, although it is correct to call me Greystone when we are in company, I would like to hear you call me Crispin.'

'Yes, Crispin,' said Clarissa miserably.

He tucked her arm in his. 'Walk a little with me,' he urged. 'We have not had a chance to be alone like this for a long time. Still, after tomorrow, we can be together all the time.'

'Yes, Grey–, I mean, Crispin.'

'The redoubtable Miss Amy Tribble arranged this meeting. Do you know why?'

'No, Crispin.'

'It is because she thinks you have bride nerves. She fears your mother talked to you about the mysteries of the marriage bed and frightened you out of your wits.'

Clarissa stopped and turned to face him. 'I am such a goose to be so afraid,' she murmured, hanging her head. 'It is something, I believe, all ladies must endure.'

'I sometimes find it in me to wonder if that mother of yours is jealous of you. Walk across the grass with me, away from the houses.'

They walked together across the large expanse of cropped grass and stood on the edge of the ha-ha. 'Why have we come here?'

asked Clarissa with a tremor in her voice.

'This, my love, is by way of being a wedding rehearsal.' He took her face between his long fingers and kissed her cold lips, his powerful arms crushing her against him. He kissed her until he felt her body begin to respond. He kissed her hair, her lips, and the tops of her breasts and then returned to her mouth again, kissing and kissing with single-minded passion until her body began to throb and pulsate.

'It will be like this,' he said softly. 'It will be like this except we will both be naked. Your skin will feel my skin, your body will belong to mine. Can you understand? For such as us who crave fulfillment, the nights will never be long enough. Only couples who enter into a marriage of convenience suffer from lust on the one side and endurance and distaste on the other.'

'I have been so afraid, Crispin,' said Clarissa softly. 'I know what you mean. I ... I ... want you.'

'And you will have all of me for the rest of your life. Not just my body, but my heart and head. Now kiss me again and let the world of gossips and troubles go away.'

'Where have they gone?' demanded Effy

Tribble, shivering with cold. She and Amy were standing out on the narrow balcony in front of the drawing room in their night-dresses and nightcaps.

'They just vanished into the blackness,' said Amy. 'Oh, Effy, what will become of us if she tells him she can't go through with it?'

'Such a powerful man,' sighed Effy. 'I am sure he will have calmed her fears. Did you ever see such shoulders on a man, Amy, or such legs?'

'Shhh!' said Amy, leaning over the balcony. 'I think they are returning. They must not see us.' The sisters stood back.

In the light above the door, they saw the two figures approaching. The earl had his arm about Clarissa's shoulders. They were moving like sleepwalkers. They paused out-side the door. The earl drew Clarissa into his arms and kissed her long and passionately. Amy and Effy hung over the balcony and watched with interest.

At last, they heard him say good night.

'Did you mark her face as she turned it up to his?' crowed Amy. 'Love and happiness! Hurray. The Tribble sisters are triumphant!'

Lady Clarendon shook her husband awake. 'What is it?' he asked in alarm. 'She set the house on fire again?'

'It's those Tribbles,' said Lady Clarendon severely. 'They must be told to leave right after the wedding. They are quite mad. They are out on the balcony in front of the drawing room in their nightgowns, cheering and dancing and cavorting up and down.'

'Probably drunk,' said the viscount. 'I'm going back to sleep.'

The wedding of the Earl of Greystone and the Honourable Clarissa Vevian was a resounding success. As soon as Effy saw Clarissa floating down the aisle to the altar, a picture of beauty and grace, she began to cry with happiness while Amy berated her for being a ninny and then burst into sentimental tears herself.

To both Mr Randolph's and Mr Haddon's consternation, the sisters cried all through the service and began to recover only when they were seated at the wedding breakfast.

The Countess Clarendon had forgiven the sisters for their odd behaviour. Clarissa looked beautiful and was behaving beautifully. But as she saw her daughter's radiant face turned up to the earl's, Lady Clarendon could not help experiencing a certain qualm of jealousy. Her own marriage had been so very sensible. She had hardly seen

Clarendon before their marriage. It had been arranged between her parents' lawyers and his.

Only when the earl and Clarissa had finally driven off did the Tribble sisters find themselves suffering from reaction.

'Clarissa said she tried very hard to find us a new client,' said Amy. 'But no one's bitten except these Kendalls, and I hear they are vulgar to a fault and terribly common.'

'But rich,' pointed out Effy.

'You're right,' said Amy with a sigh. 'We work for a living and must always remember we cannot be choosy. We'll call on them tomorrow.' She sighed again. There was a long silence.

'Of what are you thinking?' asked Effy at last.

'I am thinking of a certain pair of nabobs, and I am thinking I would like to crack their heads together,' said Amy. 'Don't they see us as *women?*'

'No, dear,' said Effy. 'But there is always hope, Amy. For any woman of any age, there is always hope.'

The publishers hope that this book has given you enjoyable reading. Large Print Books are especially designed to be as easy to see and hold as possible. If you wish a complete list of our books please ask at your local library or write directly to:

Magna Large Print Books
Magna House, Long Preston,
Skipton, North Yorkshire.
BD23 4ND

This Large Print Book, for people
who cannot read normal print,
is published under the auspices of

THE ULVERSCROFT FOUNDATION